D1391845

Enid Blyton

The Mystery of
the Pantomime Cat

Enid Blyton

The Mystery of
the Pantomime Cat

DEAN

First published in Great Britain 1949
Reissued 2004 by Dean
an imprint of Egmont UK Limited
239 Kensington High Street, London W8 6SA

Copyright © Enid Blyton Limited 2004

Enid Blyton's signature is a registered trademark of
Enid Blyton Limited. A Chorion company.

ISBN 978 0603 56173 3
ISBN 0603 56173 X

Printed and bound in Singapore

1 3 5 7 9 10 8 6 4 2

Contents

1. AT THE RAILWAY STATION

Larry and Daisy were waiting for Fatty to come and call for them with Buster the Scottie. They swung on the gate and kept looking down the road.

'Nice to be home for the hols again,' said Daisy. 'I wish Fatty would hurry up. We shan't be in time to meet Pip and Bets' train if he doesn't hurry up. I'm longing to see them again. It seems ages since the Christmas hols.'

'There he is!' said Larry, and jumped off the gate. 'And there's Buster. Hello, Fatty! We'll have to hurry or we won't be in time to meet Bets and Pip.'

'Plenty of time,' said Fatty, who never seemed in a hurry. 'Well, it'll be fun to be all together again, won't it? – the Five Find-Outers, ready to tackle the next super-colossal mystery!'

'Woof,' said Buster, feeling a bit left out. Fatty corrected himself. 'The Five Find-Outers and Dog. Sorry, Buster.'

'Come on,' said Daisy. 'The train will be in. Fancy, we've had almost a week's holiday and haven't seen Bets and Pip. I bet they didn't like staying with their Aunt Sophie – she's very strict and proper. They'll be full of pleases and thank-yous and good manners for a few days!'

'It'll wear off,' said Fatty. 'Anyone seen Old Clear-Orf these hols?'

Clear-Orf was the name the children gave to Mr Goon, the village policeman. He couldn't bear the five children, and he hated Buster, who loved to dance round the policeman's ankles in a most aggravating way. The children had solved a good many mysteries which Mr Goon had tried to work out himself, and he was very jealous of them.

'He'll say "Clear orf!" as soon as he spots one of us anywhere,' said Larry, with a grin. 'It's sort of automatic with him. I wonder if there'll be any more mysteries these hols. I feel I could just use my brains nicely on a good juicy mystery!'

The others laughed. 'Don't let Daddy hear you say that,' said Daisy. 'You had such a bad report that he'll wonder why you don't use your brains for Latin and maths instead of mysteries!'

'I suppose he had "Could use his brains better," or "Does not make the best use of his brains," on his report,' said Fatty. 'I know the sort of thing.'

'You couldn't *ever* have had those remarks put on *your* report, Fatty,' said Daisy, who had a great admiration for Fatty's brains.

'Well,' said Fatty modestly, 'I *usually* have "A brilliant term's work," or "Far surpasses the average for his form" or . . .'

Larry gave him a punch. 'Still the same modest but conceited old Fatty! It's marvellous how you manage to boast in such a modest tone of voice, Fatty. I . . .'

'Stop arguing; there's the train's whistle,' said Daisy, beginning to run. 'We simply *must* be on the platform to meet Pip and Bets. Oh, poor Buster – he's getting left behind on his short legs. Come on, Buster!'

The three children and Buster burst through the door on to the platform. Buster gave a delighted bark, and sniffed at the bottom of a pair of stout dark blue trousers, whose owner was standing by the bookstall.

There was an exasperated snort. 'Clear orf!' said

a familiar voice. 'Put that dog on a lead!'

'Oh – hello, Mr Goon!' chorused Fatty, Larry, and Daisy, as if Mr Goon was their dearest friend.

'Fancy seeing *you*!' said Fatty. 'I hope you are quite well, Mr Goon – not feeling depressed at this weather, or . . .'

Mr Goon was getting ready to be very snappish when the train came in with a thunderous roar that made it impossible to talk.

'There's Pip!' yelled Larry, and waved so violently that he almost knocked off Mr Goon's helmet. Buster retired under a platform seat and sat there looking very dignified. He didn't like trains. Mr Goon stood not far off, looking for whoever it was he had come to meet.

Bets and Pip tumbled out of the train in excitement. Bets ran to Fatty and hugged him. 'Fatty! I hoped you'd come and meet us! Hello Larry, hello Daisy!'

'Hello, young Bets,' said Fatty. He was very fond of Bets. He smacked Pip on the back. 'Hello Pip! You've just come back in time to help in a super-colossal mystery!'

This was said in a very loud voice, which was

meant to reach Mr Goon's ears. But unfortunately he didn't hear. He was shaking hands with another policeman, a young, pink-faced, smiling fellow.

'Look!' said Larry. 'Another policeman! Are we going to have two in Peterswood now, then?'

'I don't know,' said Fatty, looking hard at the second policeman. 'I rather like the look of Mr Goon's friend – he looks a nice sort of man.'

'I like the way his ears stick out,' said Bets.

'Idiot,' said Pip. 'Where's old Buster, Fatty?'

'Here, Buster – come out from under that seat,' said Fatty. 'Shame on you for being such a coward!'

Buster crawled out, trying to wag his tail while it was still down, in a most apologetic way. But as the train then began to pull out of the station again with a terrific noise, Buster retired hurriedly under the seat once more.

'Poor Buster! I'm sure if I was a dog I'd hide under a seat too,' said Bets, comfortingly.

'It's not so long ago since you always stood behind me when the train came in,' said Pip. 'And I remember you trying to . . .'

'Come on,' said Fatty, seeing Bets beginning to go red. 'Let's go. BUSTER! Come on out and don't be an idiot. The train is now a mile away.'

Buster came out, saw *two* pairs of dark blue legs walking towards him, and ran at them joyfully. Mr Goon cried out.

'That dog!' he said, balefully. He turned to his companion. 'You want to look out for this here dog,' he told him, in a loud voice. 'He wants reporting. He's not under proper control, see? You keep your eyes open for him, PC Pippin, and don't you stand no nonsense.'

'Oh, Mr Goon, don't say there's going to be *two* of you chasing poor Buster,' began Fatty, always ready for an argument with Mr Goon.

'There's *not* going to be two of us,' said Mr Goon. 'I'm off on holiday – about time too – and this here's my colleague, PC Pippin, who's coming to take over while I'm away. And I'm very glad we've seen you, because now I can point you all out to him, and tell him to keep his eye on you. *And* that dog too.' He turned to his companion, who was looking a little startled.

'See these five kids? They think themselves very clever – think they can solve all the mysteries in the district! The trouble they've put me to – you wouldn't believe it! Keep your eye on them, PC Pippin – and if there's any mystery about, keep it to yourself. If you don't, you'll have these kids poking their noses into what concerns the law, and making themselves regular nuisances.'

'Thanks for the introduction, Mr Goon,' said Fatty, with a grin. He smiled at the other policeman. 'Pleased to welcome you to Peterswood, Mr Pippin. I hope you'll be happy here. And – er – if at any time we can help you, just let us know.'

'There you are! What did I tell you?' said Mr Goon, going red in the face. 'Can't stop interfering! You clear orf, all of you, and take that pestiferous dog with you. And mind you, I shall warn PC Pippin of all your little tricks and you'll find he won't stand any nonsense. See?'

Mr Goon stalked off with his friend PC Pippin, who looked round at the children rather apologetically as he went. Fatty gave him a large wink. Pippin winked back.

'I like him,' said Bets. 'He's got a nice face. And his ears . . .'

'Stick out. Yes, you told us that before,' said Pip. 'Hey, Fatty, I bet old Mr Goon is going to have a wonderful time telling PC Pippin all about us. He'll make us out to be a band of young gangsters or something.'

'I bet he will!' said Fatty. 'I'd just love to hear what he says about us. I guess our ears will burn.'

They did burn! Mr Goon was really enjoying himself warning PC Pippin about the Five Find-Outers – and Dog!

'You keep a firm hand on them,' said Mr Goon. 'And don't you stand any nonsense from that big boy – regular pest he is.'

'I thought he looked quite a good sort,' said PC Pippin, surprised.

Mr Goon did one of his best snorts. 'That's all part of his artfulness. The times that boy's played his tricks on me – messed me up properly – given me all kinds of false clues, and spoilt some of my best cases! He's a halfwit, that's what he is – always dressing himself up and acting the fool.'

'But isn't he the boy that Inspector Jenks has got such a high opinion of?' said PC Pippin, frowning in perplexity. 'I seem to remember him saying that . . .'

This was quite the wrong remark to make to Mr

Goon. He went purple in the face and glared at PC Pippin, who looked back at him in alarm.

'That boy sucks up to Inspector Jenks,' said Mr Goon. 'See? He's a regular sucker-up, that boy is. Don't you believe a word that the Inspector says about him. And just you look out for mysterious redheaded boys dashing about all over the place, see?'

PC Pippin's eyes almost popped out of his head. 'Er – redheaded boys?' he said, in an astonished voice. 'I don't understand.'

'Use your brains, PC Pippin,' said Mr Goon in a lofty voice. 'That boy, Fatty – he's got no end of disguises, and one of his favourite ones is a red wig. The times I've seen redheaded boys! And it's been Fatty dressed up just to trick me. You be careful, PC Pippin. He'll try the same trick on you, you mark my words. He's a bad lot. All those children are pests – interfering pests. No respect for the law at all.'

PC Pippin listened in surprise, but most respectfully. Mr Goon was twice his age and must have had a lot of experience. PC Pippin was very new and very keen. He felt proud to take Mr Goon's place while he was away on holiday.

'I don't expect anything difficult will turn up while I'm away,' said Mr Goon, as they turned into the gate of his little front garden. 'But *if* something turns up, keep it to yourself, Pippin – don't let those kids get their noses into it, whatever you do – and just you send for me if they do, see? And try and get that dog run in for something. It's a dangerous dog, and I'd like to get it out of the way. You see what you can do.'

PC Pippin felt rather dazed. He had liked the children and the dog. It was surprising to find that Mr Goon had such different ideas. Still – he ought to know! PC Pippin determined to do his very best for Mr Goon. His very, very best!

2. A NICE LITTLE PLAN FOR PIPPIN

The Find-Outers were very pleased to be together again. The Easter holidays were not as long as the summer ones, and almost a week had gone by before Pip and Bets had arrived home from their stay with their aunt, so there didn't seem to be much time left.

'Not quite three weeks,' groaned Larry. 'I do hope the weather's decent. We can go for some bike rides and picnics then.'

'And there's a good little show on down at the Little Theatre,' said Daisy. 'It's a kind of skit on Dick Whittington – very funny. I've seen it already, but we might all go again.'

'Oh – is that little company still going?' said Fatty, with interest. 'I remember seeing some of its plays in the Christmas hols. Some of the acting was pretty poor. I wonder if they'd like to try *me* out in a few parts. You know, last term at school . . .'

'Fatty! *Don't* tell us you took the leading part in the school play *again*,' begged Larry. 'Doesn't anyone else *ever* take the leading part at your school but you?'

'Fatty's very, very good at acting – aren't you, Fatty?' said Bets, loyally. 'Look how he can disguise himself and take even *us* in! Fatty, are you going to disguise yourself these hols? Please do! Do you remember when you dressed up as that old balloon woman, and sold balloons?'

'And old Clear-Orf came along and wanted to see your licence,' chuckled Daisy. 'But you had so many petticoats on that you pretended you couldn't find it.'

'And Bets spotted it was you because she suddenly saw you had clean fingernails and filthy dirty hands,' said Larry, remembering. 'And that made her suspicious. I always thought that was smart of Bets.'

'You're making me feel I must disguise myself at once!' said Fatty, with a grin. 'What about playing a little joke on PC Pippin? What a lovely name!'

'Yes – and it suits him,' said Bets. 'He's got a sort of apple-cheeked face – a nice round ripe pippin.'

Everyone roared. 'You tell him that,' said Pip. 'Go up to him and say, "Dear nice round ripe pippin." He'll be *so* surprised.'

'Don't be silly,' said Bets. 'As if I would! I quite liked him.'

'I wish something would turn up while Mr Goon is away,' said Fatty. 'Wouldn't he be mad to miss a mystery! And I bet we could help PC Pippin beautifully. He'd *like* our help, I expect. He doesn't look awfully clever – actually he might not be so good at snooping about as Mr Goon, because Mr Goon's had a lot of experience, and he's older – PC Pippin looks rather young. I bet we could tackle a mystery better than he could. We've solved a lot now. Six, in fact!'

'We can't possibly expect a mystery *every* hols,' said Larry.

'Let's make up one for PC Pippin,' said Bets, suddenly. 'Just a teeny-weeny one! With clues and things. He'd get awfully excited about it.'

The others stared at her. Fatty gave a sudden grin. 'Gosh! That's rather an idea of Bets, isn't it? Larry's right when he says we can't possibly expect a mystery every hols and somehow I don't feel one will turn up in the next three weeks. So we'll concoct one – for that nice round ripe Pippin to solve!'

Everyone began to feel excited. It was something to plan and look forward to.

'I bet he'll make a whole lot of notes, and be proud to show them to Mr Goon,' said Larry. 'And I bet Mr Goon will smell a rat and know it's us. What a swizz for them!'

'Now this is really very interesting,' said Fatty, feeling pleased. 'It will be a nice little job for PC Pippin to use his brains on, it'll be some fun for us, and it will be *most* annoying for Mr Goon when he comes back – because I bet he's warned PC Pippin about us. And all he'll find is that PC Pippin has wasted his time on a pretend mystery!'

'What mystery shall we make up?' said Bets, pleased that her idea was so popular with the others. 'Let's think of a really good one – that Fatty can use disguises for. I love it when Fatty disguises himself.'

'Let's all think hard,' said Fatty. 'We want to rouse suspicions, first of all – do something that will make PC Pippin think there's something up, you know – so that he will nose about – and find a few little clues . . .'

'That we put ready for him,' said Bets, with a squeal of laughter. 'Oh *yes*! Oh, I *know* I shan't think of anything. Hurry up, everyone, and think hard.'

There was silence for a few minutes. As Bets said, she couldn't think of an idea at all.

'Well – anyone thought of anything?' asked Fatty. 'Daisy?'

'I *have* thought of something – but it's a bit feeble,' said Daisy. 'What about sending PC Pippin a mysterious letter through the post?'

'No good,' said Fatty. 'He'd suspect us at once. Larry, have *you* thought of anything?'

'Well, what about mysterious noises in PC Pippin's back garden at night?' said Larry. 'Very feeble, I know.'

'It is a bit,' said Fatty. 'Doesn't lead to anything. We want to do something that will really get PC Pippin worked up, make him think he's on to something big.'

'I can only think of something feeble too,' said Pip. 'You know – hiding in a garden at night till PC Pippin comes by – and then letting him hear us whisper – and then rushing off in the dark so that he suspects we've been up to mischief.'

'Now, there's something in *that*,' said Fatty, thinking over it. 'That really could lead on to something else. Let's see now. I'll work it out.'

Everyone was respectfully silent. They looked at Fatty as he pursed his mouth and frowned. The great brains were working!

'I think I've got it,' said Fatty, at last. 'We'll do this – I'll disguise myself as a ruffian of some kind – and I'll lend Larry a disguise too. We'll find out what PC Pippin's beat is at night – where he goes and what time – and Larry and I will hide in the garden of some empty house till he comes by.'

He paused to think, and then nodded his head. 'Yes – and as soon as we hear PC Pippin coming, we'll begin to whisper loudly so that he'll hear us and challenge us. Then we'll make a run for it as if we were scared of him and didn't want to be seen.'

'But where does all this lead to?' said Larry.

'Wait a bit and see,' said Fatty, enjoying himself. 'Now, we'll escape all right – and what will PC Pippin do? He'll go into the garden, of course, and shine his torch round – and he'll find a torn-up note!'

'Oooh, yes,' said Bets, thrilled. 'What's in the note?'

'The note will contain the name of some place

for a further meeting,' said Fatty. 'We'll think of somewhere good. And when our nice round ripe Pippin arrives at the next meeting place, he'll find some lovely clues!'

'Which we'll have put there!' said Pip, grinning. 'Oh yes, Fatty – that's fine. We'll lead PC Pippin properly up the garden path.'

'The clues will lead somewhere else,' said Fatty, beaming. 'In fact it will be a nice wild-goosechase for PC Pippin. He'll love it. And won't Mr Goon's face be a picture when he hears about it all – he'll know it's us all right.'

'When can we do it? Oh, Fatty, let's begin it soon,' begged Bets. 'Can't you and Larry begin tonight?'

'No. We have to find out what PC Pippin's beat is first,' said Fatty. 'And we've got to spot an empty house on his beat. We'd better stalk him tonight, Larry, and find out where he goes. Mr Goon always used to set off about half past seven. Can you manage to come to my house by that time?'

'Yes, I think so,' said Larry. 'We have dinner at seven. I can gobble it down and be with you all right.'

So it was decided that Larry and Fatty should stalk PC Pippin that night and see exactly what his beat was, so that the next night they could prepare their little surprise for him. Bets was thrilled. She loved an adventure like this – it didn't have the frightened excitement of a real mystery, it was under their control, and nothing horrid could come out of it, except perhaps a scolding from Mr Goon!

Larry arrived at Fatty's house at twenty-five past seven that night. It was almost dark. They were not disguised, as there was no time to dress Larry up. The two boys slipped out of Fatty's house and made their way to the street where Mr Goon's house was. PC Pippin had it now, of course.

The boys could hear the telephone ringing in PC Pippin's front room, and they could hear him answering it. Then the receiver was put down, and the light in the room went out.

'He's coming!' whispered Fatty. 'Squash up more into the bushes, Larry.'

PC Pippin walked down to his front gate. He had rubber on the soles of his boots and he did not make much noise. The boys could just see him as he turned up the street, away from them.

'Come on,' whispered Fatty. 'He's beginning

his beat. We'll see exactly where he goes.'

They followed cautiously behind PC Pippin. The policeman went down the High Street, and was very conscientious indeed about trying doors and looking to see if the windows of the shops were fastened. The boys got rather bored with so much fumbling and examining. Each time PC Pippin stopped they had to stop too and hide somewhere.

After about an hour, PC Pippin moved off again, having decided that no burglar could possibly enter any shop in the High Street that night, anyway. He shut off his torch and turned into a side street. The boys crept after him.

PC Pippin went down the street softly, and then went to examine a lock-up garage there. 'Why doesn't he get on with his beat?' groaned Larry, softly. 'All this stopping and starting!'

PC Pippin went on again. He appeared to have quite a systematic method – going up one side of the road and down the other, and then into the next road and so on. If he did this every night, it would be easy to lie in wait for him somewhere!

'It's nine o'clock,' said Fatty, in a low voice, as

he heard the church clock strike loudly. 'And we're in Willow Road. There's an empty house over the other side, Larry. We could hide in the garden there tomorrow night, just before nine. Then we could startle PC Pippin when he comes along there. Look – he's shining his torch on the gate now. Yes, that's what we'll do – hide in the garden there.'

'Good,' said Larry, with relief. 'I'm tired of dodging round like this, and the wind's really cold too. Come on – let's go home. Let's meet tomorrow morning at Pip's to tell the others what we've decided, and make our plans.'

'Right,' said Fatty, who was also very glad that the shadowing of PC Pippin was at an end. 'See you tomorrow. Sssssst! Here comes PC Pippin again.'

They squeezed themselves into the hedge and were relieved when the policeman's footsteps passed them.

'Gosh – I nearly sneezed then,' whispered Larry. 'Come on – I'm frozen.'

They went quietly home, Larry to tell Daisy, his sister, that they had found a good place to hide the next night, and Fatty to plan their disguises. He pulled out some old clothes and looked at them. Aha, PC Pippin, he thought, there's a nice little surprise being planned for you!

3. TWO RUFFIANS – AND PC PIPPIN

The five children discussed their plan with great interest the next day. Buster sat near them, ears cocked up, listening.

'Sorry, old thing, but I'm afraid you're not in this,' said Fatty, patting the little Scottie. 'You'll have to be tied up at home. Can't have you careering after me, yapping at PC Pippin, when he comes by our hiding-place.'

'Woof,' said Buster, mournfully, and lay down as if he had no further interest in the subject.

'Poor Buster,' said Bets, rubbing the sole of her shoe along his back. 'You hate to be left out, don't you? But this isn't a *real* mystery, Buster. It's only a pretend one.'

The children decided that Larry and Fatty had better get into their disguises at Larry's house, as it was near to the garden where they were to hide. Then they could sprint back to Larry's without much bother.

'I'll bring the clothes along in a suitcase after tea,' said Fatty. 'Any chance of hiding the case somewhere in your garden, Larry? In a shed or something? Grown-ups are always so suspicious of things like that. If I arrive at your house complete with suitcase your mother's quite likely to want to know what's in it.'

'Yes. Well, there's the little shed halfway down the garden,' said Larry. 'The one the gardener uses. I'll join you there whatever time you say – and we might as well change into our disguises there, Fatty. We'll be safe. What are we going to wear?'

'Oh, *can* we come and see you getting into your disguises?' said Bets, who didn't want to miss anything if she could help it. 'Pip and I could slip out when we are supposed to be reading after supper.'

'Mummy is going to the Little Theatre to see the show there tonight,' said Pip, remembering. 'We'll be quite safe to come and see you disguising yourselves.'

So, at eight o'clock that night, Fatty, Larry, Daisy, Pip, and Bets were all hiding in the little shed together. Fatty pinned a sack tightly across the tiny window so that no light would show. Then he and Larry began to disguise themselves.

'We'd better make ourselves pretty awful-looking,' said Fatty. 'I bet PC Pippin will shine that torch of his on us, and we'll let him get a good look at our ruffianly faces. Here, Larry – you wear this frightful moustache. And look, there's that red wig of mine – wear that too, under an old cap. You'll look horrible.'

Bets watched the two boys, fascinated. Fatty was extremely clever at dressing up. He had many books on the art of disguising yourself, and there wasn't much he didn't know about it! Also, he had a wonderful collection of false eyebrows, moustaches, beards, and even sets of celluloid teeth that fitted over his own teeth, and stuck out horribly.

He put on a ragged beard. He screwed up his face and applied black greasepaint to his wrinkles. He stuck on a pair of shaggy eyebrows, which immediately altered him beyond recognition. Bets gave a squeal.

'You're horrible, Fatty! I don't know you. I can't bear to look at you.'

'Well, don't then,' said Fatty, with a grin that showed black gaps in his front teeth. Bets stared in horror.

'Fatty! Where are your teeth? You've got two missing!'

'Just blacked them out, that's all,' said Fatty, with another dreadful grin. 'In this light it looks as if I've got some missing, doesn't it?'

He put on a wig of thinnish hair that straggled under his cap. He screwed up his face, and waggled his beard at Bets and Daisy.

'You look disgusting and very frightening,' said Daisy. 'I'm glad I'm not going to walk into you unexpectedly tonight. I'd be scared stiff. Oh, look at Larry, Bets – he's almost as bad as Fatty. Larry, *don't* squint like that.'

Larry was squinting realistically, and had screwed up his mouth so that his moustache was all on one side.

'Don't overdo it,' said Fatty. 'You look like an idiot now – not that that's much of a change for you.'

Larry slapped him on the back. 'You mind what you say to me,' he growled, in a deep voice. 'I'm Loopy Leonard from Lincoln.'

'You look it,' said Daisy. 'You're both horrible. PC Pippin won't believe you're real when he sees you!'

Fatty looked at Daisy. 'Do you think he'll see through our disguises then?' he asked, anxiously. 'Have we overdone it?'

'No. Not really,' said Daisy. 'I mean, a policeman sees lots of terrible ruffians and scoundrels, I expect, and some of them must look as bad as you. Ugh, you do look revolting. I shall dream about you tonight.'

'Hey – time's getting on,' said Pip, suddenly looking at his watch. He had been silent and a little sulky because he was not going too. But, as Fatty pointed out, he was not tall enough to pass for a man, whereas he and Larry were. They were both well grown, and Fatty especially was quite burly now.

'Right. We'll go,' said Fatty, and Larry opened the door of the shed cautiously.

'We'll have to go past the kitchen door,' he said. 'But it's all right, no one will hear us.'

The two horrible-looking ruffians tiptoed up the path and past the kitchen door. Just as they got there, the door opened and a bright beam of light fell on the two of them. There was a loud scream and the door was banged shut.

'Gosh! That was Janet, our cook,' whispered Daisy. 'She must have had the fright of her life when she saw you. Quick, leave before she tells Daddy!'

The two boys scurried away into the road. Bets went home with Pip. Daisy went in at the garden door and heard Janet telling her father in a most excited voice about the two frightful men she had seen. 'Great big fellows, sir,' she said, 'about six feet high, they were – and they glared at me out of piercing eyes, and growled like dogs.'

Daisy chuckled and slipped upstairs. She wasn't at all surprised at Janet's horror. Those two certainly had looked dreadful.

Fatty and Larry made their way cautiously to the empty house. They crossed over whenever they heard anyone coming along the dark streets. Nobody saw them, which was a good thing, for most people would certainly have raised the alarm at the sight of two such extraordinary-looking rogues.

They came to the empty house. They slipped in

at the front gate very quietly indeed. There was a side gate as well.

'When PC Pippin comes by, we'll start our whispering here, under this bush,' said Fatty. 'And then when he comes in at the front gate to investigate, we'll sprint out of the side gate. Let him shine his light on our faces, because he can't possibly tell who we are in these frightful disguises.'

'Right,' said Larry. 'Got the torn-up note, Fatty?'

Fatty felt in his pocket. He drew out an envelope. In it was a dirty piece of paper, torn into six or eight pieces. On it, Fatty had written a cryptic message.

Behind Little Theatre. Ten pm. Friday.

He grinned as he took out the torn pieces and thought of the message on them. 'When PC Pippin turns up behind the Little Theatre on Friday we'll see that he finds a lot of clues,' he said to Larry. He scattered the bits of paper on the ground below the bush they were hiding behind. They fell there and lay waiting for the unsuspecting PC Pippin to pick them up later on in the evening!

'Shh!' said Larry suddenly. 'He's coming. I know

his funny little cough now, though I can't hear his footsteps. Ah – now I can.'

The boys waited silently until PC Pippin was near the garden. Then Fatty said something in a sibilant whisper. Larry then rustled the bush. Fatty said, 'Ssssst!' and PC Pippin switched on his torch at once.

'Now then! Who's there? You come on out and show yourselves!' said PC Pippin's voice, sounding very sharp indeed.

'Don't run yet,' whispered Fatty. 'Let him get a look at us.'

Larry rustled the bush again. Pippin turned his torch on to it at once, and was horrified to see two such villainous faces peering out at him. What ruffians! Up to no good, *he'd* be bound!

'Run for it!' said Fatty, as the policeman swung open the front gate.

The two boys at once sprinted out of the back gate, and raced off down the road, with PC Pippin a very bad third. 'Hey, stop there! Stop!' he shouted. This was more than the boys had bargained for! Suppose somebody *did* stop them! It would be very awkward indeed.

But, fortunately, no one stopped them or even

tried to, though the village butcher, out for a walk with his wife on the fine spring night, did step out to catch hold of them. But when he saw Fatty's horrible-looking face in the light of a street lamp he thought better of it, and the boys raced by in safety.

They turned in at Larry's gate thankfully. They went to the little shed and sank down, panting. Fatty grinned.

'Nice work, Larry! He'll go back there with his torch and snoop round – and he'll find the torn bits of paper and turn up on time for his next clues on Friday. I enjoyed that. Did you?'

'Yes,' said Larry. 'I only wish I didn't have to take off this great disguise. Can't we go round the town a bit and show ourselves to a few more people?'

'Better not,' said Fatty. 'Come on – let's take these things off. Hey – I wish it had been old Mr Goon who came along and spotted us – what a thrill for him!'

Meanwhile, PC Pippin had made his way back to the garden where the two ruffians had been hiding. He was excited. He had never hoped for anything to happen while he was taking Goon's place. And now he had surprised two horrible-looking villains hiding in the garden of an empty house, no doubt planning a burglary of some kind.

PC Pippin shone his torch on the ground under the bush where the two ruffians had stood. He hoped to see some footprints there. Aha, yes – there were plenty! And there was something else too – torn pieces of paper! Could those fellows have dropped them?

PC Pippin took his notebook from his pocket and placed the bits of paper carefully in the flap at the back. There were eight pieces – with writing on them! He would examine them carefully at home. Next he took out a folding ruler and carefully measured the footprints in the soft earth. Then he looked about for cigarette-ends or any other clue. But, except for the bits of paper, there was nothing.

PC Pippin was up past midnight piecing together the bits of paper, making out the thrilling message, writing out a description of the two men, and trying to draw the footprints to measure. He felt very important and pleased. This was his first case. He was going to handle it well. He would go to that

Little Theatre on Friday night, long before ten – and see what he would find there! All this might be very, very important.

4. PLENTY OF REDHEADS – AND PLENTY OF CLUES!

The five children chuckled over the trick they had played on the unsuspecting PC Pippin. Larry had met him the morning after, and stopped to have a few words with him.

Mr Pippin, remembering Mr Goon's words of warning about the five children, looked at him rather doubtfully. This wasn't the dangerous boy though – it was one of the others.

'Good morning, Mr Pippin,' said Larry politely. 'Settled in all right?'

'Of course,' said Mr Pippin. 'Nice place, Peterswood. I've always liked it. You at home for the Easter holidays?'

'Yes,' said Larry. 'Er – discovered any mystery yet, Mr Pippin?'

'Shouldn't tell you if I had,' said Mr Pippin, grinning at Larry. 'I've had a warning about you, see?'

'Yes. We thought you probably would have,' said Larry. 'By the way, our cook had a fright last night. Said she saw two ruffians outside our back door.'

Mr Pippin pricked up his ears at once. 'Did she? What were they like?'

'Well – she said one of them had red hair,' said Larry. 'But you'd better ask her if you want any particulars. Why? Have *you* seen them?'

'Perhaps I have and perhaps I haven't,' said Mr Pippin, annoyingly.

He nodded to Larry and walked off. He was thinking hard. So Larry's cook had also seen a red-haired ruffian. Must have been the same red-haired man that he too had seen that night then. What were they up to? He decided to interview Larry's cook, and did so. He came away with a very lurid account of two enormous villains, six feet high at least, growling and groaning, squinting and pulling faces.

One of them certainly had red hair. Mr Pippin began to look out for people with red hair. When he met Mr Kerry the cobbler, who had flaming red hair, he eyed him with such suspicion that Mr Kerry felt really alarmed.

PC Pippin also came across the vicar's brother, a kind and harmless tricyclist who liked to ride three times round the village each morning for exercise. When Mr Pippin had met him for the third time, and scrutinised him very very carefully, the vicar's brother began to think something must be wrong. Mr Pippin was also surprised – how many more times was he going to see this red-haired tricyclist?

When Larry related to the others that he had met PC Pippin, and told him about the red-haired man seen by the cook, and when Fatty heard from Janet the cook that the policeman had actually been to interview her about him, he chuckled.

'I think a spot of disguising is indicated,' he said to the others. 'A few red-haired fellows might interest our nice round ripe Pippin.'

So at twelve o'clock, a red-haired telegraph boy appeared on a bicycle, whistling piercingly. When he saw Mr Pippin he stopped and asked him for directions to an address he didn't know. The policeman looked at him. Another red-haired fellow! There was no end to them in Peterswood, it seemed.

At half past one, another red-haired fellow

appeared beside the surprised PC Pippin. This time, he was a man with a basket. He had black eyebrows which looked rather odd with his red hair, and frightful teeth that stuck out in front. He talked badly because of these.

'Scuthe me,' lisped the red-haired fellow. 'Pleathe, can you thay where the Potht Offith ith?'

At first PC Pippin thought the fellow was talking in a foreign language, but at last discovered that he was merely lisping. He looked at him closely. *Another* red-haired man! Most peculiar. None of them really looked like the ruffian he had seen the night before though.

At half past two, yet another red-haired fellow knocked at PC Pippin's door, and delivered a newspaper which he said must have been left at the wrong house. Pippin thought it was one that Mr Goon had delivered and thanked him. He stared at him, frowning. All this red hair! Fatty stared back unwinkingly.

Feeling uncomfortable, though he didn't know why, PC Pippin shut the door and went back into the front room. He felt that if he saw one more red-haired man that day he would really go to the optician and see if there was something wrong with his eyes!

And at half past five, when he was setting out to go to the post office, what did he see but an elderly looking man shuffling along with a stick – and with bright red hair sticking out from under his cap!

I'm seeing things, thought poor Mr Pippin to himself, I've got red hair on the brain.

Then a memory struck him. Well! What was it that Mr Goon told me? He warned me against red-haired fellows dashing about all over the place, didn't he? What did he mean? What's all this red-haired business? Oh yes – Mr Goon said it would be Fatty disguising himself! But that boy *couldn't* be as clever as all that! Mr. Pippin began to review all the red-haired people he had seen that day. He thought with great suspicion about the man he had seen three times on a tricycle.

Ah! Wait till I meet the next redhead, said Mr Pippin darkly to himself. If there's tricks played on *me*, I can play a few too! I'll give the next redhead a real fright!

It so happened that the next one he met was the vicar's brother on his tricycle again, hurrying along to catch the post at the post office. Mr Pippin stepped out into the road in front of him.

The vicar's brother rang his bell violently but Mr Pippin didn't get out of the way. So the rider put on his brakes suddenly, and came to such a sudden stop that he almost fell off.

'What is it, constable?' said the vicar's brother, astonished. 'I nearly ran you down.'

'What's your name and address, please?' asked Mr Pippin, taking out his notebook.

'My name is Theodore Twit, and my address is the Vicarage,' said Mr Twit, with much dignity.

'Oh *yes*,' said Mr Pippin. ' "The Vicarage" I *don't* think! You can't put me off *that* way!'

Mr Twit wondered if the policeman was mad. He looked at him anxiously. Mr Pippin mistook his anxious look for fright. He suddenly clutched at Mr Twit's abundant, red hair.

'Ow!' said Mr Twit, and almost fell off his tricycle. 'Constable! What does this mean?'

Mr Pippin had been absolutely certain that the red hair would come off in his hand. When it didn't, he was horrified. He stared at Mr Twit, his pink face going a deep red.

'Do you feel all right, constable?' asked Mr Twit, rubbing his head where Mr Pippin had snatched at his hair. 'I don't understand. Oh – thank goodness, here is my sister. Muriel, do come here and tell this constable who I am. He doesn't seem to believe me.'

Mr Pippin saw a very determined-looking lady coming towards him. 'What is it, Theodore?' said the lady, in a deep, barking kind of voice. Mr Pippin took one look at Muriel, muttered a few words of shamed apology, and fled. He left behind him two very puzzled people.

'Mad,' said Muriel, in her barking voice. 'Mr Goon was mad enough, goodness knows – but really, when it comes to this man snatching at your hair, Theodore, the world must be coming to an end!'

It so happened that Miss Twit went to call on Fatty's mother that evening, and when Fatty heard her relate the story of how that extraordinary Mr Pippin had tried to snatch at dear Theodore's red hair, he had such a fit of the giggles that his mother sent him out of the room in disgust at his manners. Fatty enjoyed his laugh all to himself, with Buster gazing at him in wonder.

So old PC Pippin is on to that trick, is he? thought Fatty. Right. It must be dropped. Hope he doesn't associate me with the red-haired ruffian he saw last night, though. He won't turn up at the Little Theatre and find his precious clues if he thinks it's a trick.

The five children had had a meeting that day, which was Thursday, to decide what clues they would spread for Pippin at the back of the Little Theatre. There was a kind of verandah there, under cover, where all kinds of clues might be put.

'Cigarette-ends, of course, to make PC Pippin think other meetings have taken place there,' said Fatty.

'Yes – and matches,' said Larry. 'And what about a hanky with an initial on it – always very helpful that, when you want clues!'

'Oh yes,' said Daisy. 'I've got an old torn hanky and I'll work an initial on it. What shall I put?'

'Z,' said Fatty, promptly. 'Might as well give him something to puzzle his brains over.'

'Z!' said Bets. 'But there aren't any names beginning with Z, surely?'

'Yes there are – Zebediah and Zacharias, to start

with!' grinned Fatty. 'We'll have old PC Pippin hunting round for Zebediahs before he's very much older!'

'Well, I'll put a Z on then,' said Daisy. 'I'll get my needle and thread now. What other clues will you leave?'

'A page out of a book,' said Pip. 'Out of a timetable or something.'

'Yes. That's good,' said Fatty, approvingly. 'Any other ideas?'

'What else do people drop by accident?' wondered Daisy. 'Oh, I know what we could do. If there's a nail or anything there, we could take along a bit of cloth and jab it on the nail! Then it would look as if whoever had been there for a meeting had caught his coat on the nail. That would be a very valuable clue, if it was a real one!'

'Yes, it would,' agreed Fatty. 'And we'll take a pencil and sharpen it there – leave bits of pencil-shavings all over the place. Gosh, what a wonderful lot of clues!'

'We must also leave something to make PC Pippin go on with the chase somewhere else,' said Larry.

'Yes. What about underlining a train in the timetable page that we're going to throw down?' said Pip. 'We're going to chuck one down, aren't we? Well, if we underline a certain train – say a Sunday train – old PC Pippin will turn up for that too!'

Everyone giggled. 'And Fatty could dress up in some disguise, and slip a message into PC Pippin's hand to suggest the next place to go to,' said Daisy. 'We could send him over half the country at this rate!'

'Wait till Mr Goon gets a report of all this,' said Fatty with a grin. 'He'll see through it at once – and won't he be mad!'

Soon all the clues were ready, even to the pencil-shavings, which were in an envelope.

'When shall we place the clues?' said Bets. 'Can I come too?'

'Yes. We'll all go,' said Fatty. 'I don't see why not. There's nothing suspicious about us all going out together. We can go on our bicycles and put them in the car-park at the back of the Little Theatre. Then we'll pretend to be looking at the posters there, and one of us can slip up to the verandah and drop the clues. It won't take a minute.'

'When shall we go?' asked Bets again. She always wanted to do things at once.

'Not today,' said Fatty. 'There's a bit of a breeze. We don't want the clues blown right off the verandah. The wind may have died down by tomorrow. We'll cycle along after tea tomorrow, about six.'

So the next day, about ten to six, the five set off, with Buster as usual in Fatty's bicycle basket. They cycled round to the back of the Little Theatre and came to the car-park there. A good many children were there already, getting bicycles from the stand.

'Hello!' said Fatty, surprised. 'Has there been a show here this afternoon?'

'Yes,' said a boy nearby. 'Just a show for us children from Farleigh Homes. They let us in for nothing. It was very good. I liked the cat the best.'

'The cat? Oh, Dick Whittington's cat, you mean,' said Fatty, remembering that the show that week was supposed to be a skit on the Dick Whittington pantomime. 'It's not a real cat, is it?'

'Course not!' said the boy. Daisy, who had already seen the show, explained to Fatty.

'It's a man in a cat's skin, idiot. Must be rather a small man – or maybe it's a boy! He was very funny, I thought.'

'Look – there go the actors,' said a little girl, and she pointed to a side door. 'See, that's Dick Whittington, that pretty girl. Why do they always have a girl for the boy in pantomime? And that's Margot, who is Dick's sweetheart in the play. And there's Dick's master – and his mother, look – she's a man really, as you can see. And there's the captain of Dick's ship – isn't he fine? And there's the chief of the islands that Dick visits.'

The five children gazed at the actors as they left the side door of the Little Theatre. They all looked remarkably ordinary.

'Where's the cat?' asked Bets.

'He doesn't seem to have gone with them,' said the little girl. 'Anyway, I wouldn't know what he was like, because he wore his cat-skin all the time. He was awfully good. I loved him.'

A teacher called loudly, 'Irene! Donald! What are you keeping us waiting for? Come on at once.'

The car-park emptied. Fatty looked round. 'Now,' he said, 'come on! The coast is clear. We'll all go and look at these posters and talk to one another – and then when we are sure no one is watching us, I'll slip up to the verandah and drop the clues.'

It was most annoying, however, because one or two people kept coming to the car-park, and for some reason or other walked across it. Fatty finally discovered that it was a short cut to a newsagents in the next street.

'Blow!' he said. 'We'll have to hang about till it shuts. It's sure to shut soon.'

It was boring having to wait so long and talk endlessly about the posters. But at last the shop apparently did shut and nobody else took the short cut across the car-park. It was now getting dark. Fatty slipped up the three steps to the verandah.

He threw down the clues – cigarette-ends and matches – torn hanky with Z on – pencil-shavings – page torn from a timetable with one Sunday train underlined – and a bit of navy blue cloth which he jabbed hard on a nail.

He turned to go – but before he went, he took a look in at the window nearby. And what a shock Fatty got!

5. PC PIPPIN ON THE JOB

A very large, furry animal was inside the window, looking mournfully up at him – or so it seemed. The eyes were big and glassy, and gave Fatty the creeps. He recoiled back from the window, and almost fell down the verandah steps.

'What's up?' asked Larry, surprised.

'There's something peculiar up there,' said Fatty. 'Horrible big animal, looking out of the window at me. I could just see it in the faint reflection cast by that street lamp outside the car-park.'

Bets gave a little squeal. 'Don't! I'm frightened!'

'Idiot, Fatty! It must be the cat-skin of Dick Whittington's cat,' said Larry, after a moment. Everyone felt most relieved.

'Well – I suppose it was,' said Fatty, feeling very foolish. 'I never thought of that. The thing looked so lifelike though. I don't think it was just a *skin*. I think the actor who plays the cat must have still been inside it.'

'Gracious. Does he *live* in it then?' said Daisy. 'Let's go and see if it's still there, looking out of the window.'

'We'll wait here,' said Bets to Daisy.

'*We'll* go,' said Larry. 'Come on, Fatty, come on, Pip.'

The three boys stepped quietly up the verandah steps, and looked in at the window. The cat was no longer there, but as they stood watching, they saw it come in at the door of the room and run across on all fours to the fireplace. An electric fire was burning, and the boys could distinctly see the cat pretending to wash its face, rubbing its ears with its paws, in exactly the same way as a cat does.

'There it is!' said Fatty. 'It's seen us! That's why it's acting up like this. It thinks we're children who came to see the show, and it's still pretending to be Dick Whittington's cat. Gracious – it gave me a start when I first saw it at the window.'

'Meeow,' said the cat loudly, turning towards the window, and waving a paw.

'I somehow don't like it,' said Pip. 'I don't know why. But I just don't. I know it's only somebody inside the skin, but it looks too real for me. Let's go!'

They went back to the girls. It was not quite dark, and the church clock struck seven o'clock as they went to fetch their bicycles from the stands.

'Well – we've planted the clues,' said Fatty, feeling more cheerful as he undid Buster from where he had tied him to the stand. 'Hey, Buster, old chap – good thing you didn't spot that cat. You'd have thought you were seeing things – a cat as big as that!'

'Woof,' said Buster, dolefully. He didn't like being left out of the fun, and he knew something exciting had been happening. He was lifted into Fatty's basket, and then the five cycled slowly home.

'I wonder when PC Pippin will go along,' said Fatty, as he dismounted at his gate. 'He'll be sure to get there long before ten, so that he can hide before the meeting takes place – and there won't be a meeting after all! Only plenty of clues for him to find.'

'See you tomorrow, Fatty!' called Pip and Bets. 'Good-bye, Larry and Daisy. We'll have to hurry or we'll get into trouble.'

They all rode away. Fatty went indoors, thinking

of the way the cat had looked at him through the window. That really had given him a jolt! 'If I were Bets I'd dream about that!' he thought. 'I wonder if PC Pippin's going to hide himself on the verandah somewhere. If he gets a glimpse of that cat, he'll get the fright of his life.'

PC Pippin did not go to the verandah until about half past eight. He meant to be there in good time for the meeting, whatever it was. He had been very thrilled indeed to find the message about the meeting at ten o'clock behind the Little Theatre, when he had pieced together the torn bits of paper.

Mr Goon would be pleased with him if he could unearth some mystery or plot, he was sure. Pippin meant to do his best. He had already snooped round the back of the Little Theatre the day before, to see where he could hide on the night. He had discovered a hole in the verandah roof through which he could climb, and then he could sit on the windowsill of the room above, and hear everything.

Pippin arrived at the verandah as the clock on the church chimed half past eight, exactly an hour and a half after the children had left. He had his torch with him, but did not put it on until he had made sure that there was nobody about anywhere. There was a glow in the room behind the verandah. Pippin looked into the room. He saw that the glow came from an electric fire. In front of it, lying as if asleep, was what looked like a most enormous cat. PC Pippin jumped violently when he saw such a big creature.

He couldn't believe his eyes. *Was* it a cat? Yes – there were its ears – and there was its tail lying beside it on the hearth-rug.

PC Pippin gazed into the window at the great, furry creature outlined by the glow of the fire. It couldn't be a gorilla, could it? No, people wouldn't be allowed to keep a gorilla like that. Besides, it looked more like a cat than anything else.

PC Pippin was just about to give a loud exclamation when he stopped himself in time. Of course! It must be Dick Whittington's cat – the one that acted in the skit in the pantomime. He hadn't seen it himself, but he had heard about it. Funny the cat keeping its skin on like that – because there was really somebody inside it. You'd think he'd want to take the hot skin off as soon as he could!

Pippin wondered if the meeting, whatever it

was, would take place if there was that cat in the room nearby. But perhaps the meeting would be in the car-park. In that case, would it do much good him climbing on the verandah roof? He wouldn't hear a thing.

Pippin debated with himself. He cautiously switched on his torch and flashed it round the verandah floor. And he saw the clues!

His eyes brightened as he saw the cigarette-ends, the matches, and the pencil-shavings. Somebody had been here before – quite often too, judging by the cigarette-ends. The verandah must certainly be the meeting-place. Perhaps the cat was in the plot too. That was certainly an idea!

Carefully Pippin picked up the cigarette-ends, the matches, and even the pencil-shavings. He put them all into envelopes. He then found the torn timetable page, blown against the side of the verandah, and was extremely interested in the underlined Sunday train.

He looked round and found the handkerchief with Z on it, and wondered if it could be the letter N sideways. Pippin could not for the life of him think of any name beginning with Z, not even the ones the children had thought of!

Then he spotted the bit of navy blue cloth caught on a nail. Aha! Oho! *That* was the most valuable clue of all. Find somebody with a hole in a navy blue coat and you were getting somewhere!

Pippin took another cautious look into the window of the room at the back of the verandah. The great cat was still lying in front of the electric fire. Very strange – especially if you considered that the cat wasn't really a cat but a human being inside a cat-skin – or a furry skin of some sort. As he watched, Pippin saw the cat move a little, get more comfortable and apparently settle itself to sleep again.

'Funny creature,' thought Pippin, still puzzled, but very much relieved to see the cat move. 'I sort of feel that if a mouse ran across the room, the cat would be after it – though I know it's not a real cat!'

He decided that it was about time he climbed up through the hole in the verandah roof, and sat on the windowsill of the room above. The men might come any moment now – one of them might be early – you never knew! It wouldn't do for him to be seen.

With all his clues safely in his pocket, PC Pippin heaved himself up through the hole in the roof. He felt his way to the windowsill and sat down on it. It was hard and cold, and much too narrow to be comfortable. Pippin resigned himself to a long and uneasy wait.

He had not been there more than a few moments when he heard a very weird sound. PC Pippin stiffened and listened. It sounded to him very like a groan. But where could it be coming from? The room behind him was in black darkness. There was nobody near him out of doors as far as he knew – and if it was the cat before the fire making a noise, how could he *possibly* hear that? He couldn't!

The noise came again, and Pippin felt most peculiar. There he was, sitting on a narrow windowsill in the dark, waiting for rogues to meet down below – and groans sounding all round him! He didn't like it at all.

He listened, holding his breath. The groan came again. It was *behind* him! PC Pippin suddenly felt sure of that. Well, then, it must be in the *room* behind him! PC Pippin felt round the window, meaning to open it. But it was shut and fastened from inside.

Pippin remembered his torch. He took it from his belt and switched it on, so that the light shone into the room behind. Its beam swung slowly round the room – and then came to rest on something very surprising.

A man was sitting at a desk. He had fallen forward, his face on his outstretched arms. Beside him was a cup, overturned in its saucer, the spoon nearby on the table. PC Pippin stared in horror.

Then the beam picked out something else. A big wall-mirror was standing on the floor, reflecting the light of the torch. A large hole showed in the wall nearby, the place from which the mirror had been removed. A safe had been built in behind the mirror – but it was now empty, and the safe-door was swinging open.

'Thieves! A robbery!' said PC Pippin, and rose to the occasion at once. He doubled his hand in folds of his big handkerchief and drove his fist through the window! PC Pippin was on the job!

6. A MYSTERY BEGINS

The five children knew nothing about PC Pippin's exciting night, of course. Pip and Bets were asleep in bed when he smashed the window at the back of the Little Theatre, and Larry and Daisy had been told they could listen to the nine o'clock news, and then go to bed. Fatty had been in his room trying out a wonderful new aid to disguise – little pads to put inside the cheeks to make them fat!

I'll try these tomorrow, thought Fatty, with a grin. I'll put them in before breakfast and see if anyone notices.

Fatty went to bed wondering if PC Pippin had found the clues he had spread about the verandah, and how long he had waited for the mythical meeting. Poor old Pippin – he might have waited a long time!

If Fatty had only known what was happening he would never have gone off so peacefully to bed that night – he would have been snooping round the Little Theatre, looking for *real* clues! But all he had done was to play a trick on PC Pippin that had placed that gentleman right on the spot – the very spot where a burglary had taken place not so long before. Lucky Pippin!

Next day at breakfast, Fatty put in his new aid to disguise – the cheek-pads that forced out the soft part of his cheeks and made him look plump. His father, buried behind his paper, didn't seem to notice any difference. But his mother was puzzled. Fatty looked different. What was it that made him look strange? It was his cheeks! They were quite blown out.

'Frederick – have you got toothache?' his mother suddenly asked. 'Your cheeks are very swollen.'

'Oh no, Mummy,' said Fatty. 'My teeth are quite all right.'

'Well, you don't seem to be eating as much as usual, which is very strange, and certainly your cheeks look swollen,' persisted his mother. 'I shall ring up and make an appointment with the dentist.'

This was really very alarming. Fatty didn't want the dentist poking round his mouth and finding holes in his teeth. He felt quite certain that even if there wasn't a hole, the dentist would make one with that nasty scrapey instrument of his.

'Mummy – do believe me – not one of my teeth has holes in,' said Fatty, desperately. 'I ought to know.'

'Well, then, why are your cheeks so puffed out?' asked his mother, who never could leave a subject alone once she had really started on it. She turned to his father. 'Don't *you* think Frederick's cheeks are swollen?'

His father glanced up in an absent-minded manner. 'Might be,' he said. 'Eaten too much.' Then to Fatty's relief he went on reading his newspaper.

'I'll ring up the dentist immediately after breakfast,' said Fatty's mother.

In desperation, Fatty put his hands to his mouth and removed two cheek-pads – but instead of being pleased that his cheeks were now no longer swollen, his mother cried out in disgust. 'Frederick! How *can* you behave like that! Removing food from your mouth with your fingers! What *is* the matter with you this morning? You'd better leave the table.'

Before Fatty could explain about the cheek-pads, his father gave an exclamation. 'Well, well! Listen to this in the paper. "Last night it was disclosed that the manager of the Little Theatre, in Peterswood, Bucks, was found drugged in his office, and the safe in the wall behind him was open, the contents having been stolen. The police already have one suspect in their hands." '

Fatty was so astounded to hear this that he absent-mindedly put his cheek-pads into his mouth, thinking they were bits of bread, and began to chew them. He simply couldn't believe the news. Why, he and the others had actually been hanging round the Little Theatre half the evening, and they had seen nothing at all – except the pantomime cat!

'Could I see the piece, Dad?' asked Fatty, wondering why the bread in his mouth was so tough. He suddenly realised that it wasn't bread – ugh, how horrible, he had been chewing his cheek-pads! And now he didn't dare to remove them again in case his mother accused him of disgusting manners once more. It was very awkward.

'Don't talk with your mouth full, Frederick,' said

his mother. 'And of course you can't have your father's paper. You can read it when he has finished with it.'

Very fortunately at that moment the telephone rang. The maid answered it and came to fetch Fatty's mother. So Fatty was able to remove the half-chewed cheek-pads and put them into his pocket. He decided never to wear them again at mealtimes. He glanced longingly at his father's paper. Ah – he had folded it over again and the bit about the robbery was on the back, but upside down. Fatty managed to read it two or three times. He began to feel very excited.

Would it be a mystery? Suppose they hadn't got the right suspect? Then the Five Find-Outers could get on to it at once. Fatty felt that he couldn't possibly eat any more breakfast. He slid away quietly from the table before his mother came back. His father didn't notice him go.

Fatty flew off to Pip's at once. Larry and Daisy would be along soon, for they had planned a meeting there. Pip and Bets had a fine big playroom of their own, where they were not often disturbed, and it made a very good meeting place.

Pip and Bets had heard nothing of the great news. Fatty told them, and they were amazed. 'What! A robbery committed last night at the Little Theatre! Did it happen while we were there?' cried Pip, in excitement. 'Here's Larry, with Daisy. Larry, heard the news about the Little Theatre robbery?'

Larry and Daisy had heard all about it. They knew even more than Fatty because Janet, their cook, knew the woman who cleaned the Little Theatre, and had got some news from her, which she had passed on to Larry and Daisy. Larry said Janet felt certain that the robbers were the two ruffians she had seen the other night in the beam of light from the kitchen door!

'To think we were all there last night, mooching round, hanging about and everything!' groaned Fatty. 'And we never saw a thing. We were so busy preparing clues for old PC Pippin that we never saw anything of a real crime that must have been going on almost under our noses.'

'Janet says that Mrs Trotter, the woman who cleans the Little Theatre, told her that last night the police found the manager stretched out across his office desk, his head on his arms, asleep from some drug – and behind him was his empty safe,' said Larry. 'It was one that was built in the wall, hidden by a big wall-mirror hanging in front of it. She said the police must have discovered the whole thing not very long after it was done.'

'The police! I suppose that means PC Pippin,' said Fatty. 'Gosh – to think we planted him there on that verandah, surrounded by a whole lot of false clues – and there he was right on the spot when a real robbery was committed! It's absolutely maddening. If only we'd snooped round a bit more, *we* might have hit on the mystery ourselves. As it is, we've presented it to the police – or rather to PC Pippin – and they will get in straight away, and solve the whole thing.'

There was a doleful silence. It did seem very bad luck.

'I suppose PC Pippin will think all those cigarette-ends and hanky and so on are real clues now – clues to the real robbers, I mean,' said Bets, after a long pause.

'Gosh! So he will! He'll be right off on the wrong track,' said Fatty. 'That's awkward. Very awkward. I don't mind playing a silly trick on either Mr Goon or PC Pippin – but I wouldn't want to do anything that would prevent them from catching the burglars. Those clues of ours will certainly confuse them a bit.'

'You mean – they'll start looking for people whose names begin with Z, and they'll go and watch that Sunday train?' said Daisy. 'Instead of going on the right trail.'

'Yes,' said Fatty. 'Well – I think I'd better go and see PC Pippin, and own up. I don't want to set him off on the wrong track – make him waste his time solving a pretend mystery when he's got a real one to see to. Blow! It will be very awkward, having to explain. And I bet he won't give me any information either, because he'll be so annoyed with me for playing a trick on him. We could have worked nicely with old PC Pippin. We never could work with Mr Goon.

Everyone felt very glum. To think they had gone and spoilt a perfectly super *real* mystery by making up a stupid pretend one!

'I'll come with you to explain,' said Larry.

'No,' said Fatty. 'I take the responsibility for this. I'd like to keep the rest of you out of it – if PC Pippin takes it into his head to complain about us, my parents won't take a lot of notice – but yours will, Larry – and as for Pip's parents, they'll go right off the deep end.'

'They always do,' said Pip. His parents were very strict with him and Bets, and had been very much annoyed three or four times already when Mr Goon had complained to them about the children. 'I don't want our parents to know a thing. Mummy already said she's glad Mr Goon is away because now perhaps we won't get into any mischief these holidays, and make Mr Goon come round and grumble about us.'

'I'll go and see PC Pippin now,' said Fatty, getting up. 'Nothing like getting a nasty thing done at once. I do hope Pippin won't mind too much. Actually I think he's rather nice. He'll be thrilled at getting a case like this when Mr Goon is away.'

He went out, with Buster close at his heels. He whistled loudly to show that he didn't care about anything in the world. But actually Fatty did care quite a lot this morning. He felt guilty about all those false clues. He could have kicked himself for spoiling his chance of working with PC Pippin. Mr

Pippin wasn't like Mr Goon. He looked sensible, and Fatty felt sure he would have welcomed his help.

He came to Mr Goon's house, in which PC Pippin was now living while Mr Goon was away. To his surprise, the door was wide open. Fatty walked in to find PC Pippin.

There was a loud voice talking in the front room. Fatty stopped as if he had been shot. It was Mr Goon's voice. *Mr Goon*! Had he come back then? Was he going to take over the mystery? Blow!

Fatty stood there, wondering what to do. He wasn't going to confess to PC Pippin in front of Mr Goon! That would be very, very foolish. Mr Goon might even take it into his head to go and tell Inspector Jenks, the children's very great friend – and somehow Fatty felt that the Inspector would not approve of the little trick they had played on the unsuspecting PC Pippin.

Mr Goon was evidently very angry. His voice was raised, and he was going for poor PC Pippin unmercifully. Fatty couldn't help hearing as he stood in the passage, undecided whether to go in or out.

'Why didn't you send for me when you first saw

those rogues under that bush in the garden? Why didn't you tell me about the torn-up note? Didn't I tell you to let me know if anything happened? Turnip-head! Dolt! Soon as I go away they put in a dud like you, who hasn't even got the sense to send for his superior when something happens!'

Fatty decided to go – but Buster decided differently. Aha! That was the voice of his old enemy, wasn't it? With a joyful bark Buster pushed open the door of the sitting-room with his black nose, and bounded in!

7. GOON – PIPPIN – AND FATTY

There was a loud exclamation from Goon. 'That dog! Where did it come from? Clear orf, you! Ah, you'd go for my ankles, would you?'

Fatty rushed into the room at once, afraid that Mr Goon would hurt Buster. Pippin was standing by the window, looking very crestfallen indeed. Goon was by the fireplace, kicking out at Buster, who was dancing happily round his feet.

Goon looked up and saw Fatty. 'Oh, you're here too, are you?' he said. 'Setting your dog on me again! What with having to deal with that turnip-head over there, and this dratted dog, and you, it's enough to make a man retire from the police force!'

To Fatty's horror, he caught up the poker and shook it at Buster. Fatty ran to Mr Goon and twisted the poker out of his hand. The boy was white with fury.

'See?' said Goon, turning to Pippin, who was

also looking rather white. 'See that? You're a witness, you are – that boy sets his dog on me, and when I protect myself, as I've a right to do, the boy comes and assaults me. You're a witness, Pippin. Write it all down. Go on. I've been after this pest of a boy and his dog for a long time – and now I've got him. You saw it all, didn't you, Pippin?'

Fatty now had Buster in his arms. He could not trust himself to speak. He knew Mr Goon to be a stupid, ignorant man with a turn for cruelty, but Mr Goon had never shown his real nature quite so openly before.

Pippin said nothing at all. He stood by the window, looking scared and very much taken aback. He had been shouted at by Mr Goon for half an hour, blamed for all kinds of things, called all kinds of names – and now he was supposed to take out his notebook and put down a lot of untruths about that nice dog and his master.

'Pippin! Will you please write down what I tell you?' stormed Goon. 'I'll have that dog destroyed. I'll have this boy up before the court. I'll . . .'

Buster growled so fiercely that Goon stopped. 'Look here,' said Fatty, 'if you're going to do all that,

I think I'll put Buster down and let him have a real good go at you, Mr Goon. He may as well be hanged for a sheep as for a lamb. He hasn't bitten you, as you very well know – but if you're going to say he has, well then, he jolly well *can*.'

And Fatty made as if he was going to put the barking, struggling Buster down on the floor!

Goon calmed down at once, and tried to get back control of himself. He turned in a dignified way to Pippin. 'I'll tell you what to put down. Come on now, stir yourself – standing there like a ninny!'

'I'm not going to put down anything but the truth,' said Pippin, most surprisingly. 'You tormented that dog with the poker – might have injured him for life. I don't approve of behaviour of that sort, no, not even from a police officer. I like dogs – they never go for *me*. I wouldn't have that dog destroyed for anything. And all the boy did was to take the poker from you to stop you hitting his dog! A good thing he did too. You might have killed the dog – and then where would you be? In a very awkward position, Mr Goon, that's where!'

There was a dead silence after this unexpected and remarkable speech. Even Buster was quiet.

Everyone was most surprised to hear this speech from the quiet PC Pippin, and perhaps Pippin himself was most surprised of all. Goon couldn't believe his ears. He stared at Pippin with his mouth wide open, and his eyes bulged more than ever. Fatty was thrilled. Good old PC Pippin!

Goon found his tongue at last. His face was now a familiar purple. He advanced to Pippin and shook a fat and rather dirty finger under his nose.

'You'll hear more of this, see? I'm back again and I'm in charge of Peterswood now. *I'll* take charge of this new case – and you'll have nothing to do with it whatever. Nothing. If you thought you'd get a good mark for it from the Inspector, you can think again. I'll make a bad report out on you and your behaviour – thinking you'd manage it by yourself and get all the praise – not letting me know anything. Gah!'

Pippin said nothing, but looked thoroughly miserable. Fatty was very sorry for him. Goon was enjoying ticking off Pippin in front of Fatty. It gave him a sense of power, and he loved that.

'You hand me over all them clues,' said Goon. 'Every one of them. Aha! Frederick Trotteville would very much like to know what they are – wouldn't you? But you won't know! You'll never know!'

Pippin handed over to Mr Goon all the false clues that Fatty had put on the verandah! They were in envelopes or paper so Fatty could not see them – but he knew very well what they were! In fact, he could have given Mr Goon quite a lot of information about them. He grinned to himself. Right! Let Mr Goon have them and work on them. Much good would they do him! Served him right for being so beastly to PC Pippin.

'See what happens to people who work against me, instead of with me?' said Goon to Fatty, spitefully. 'I shan't let him have anything to do with this new case – and you kids won't neither! I'll manage it myself. Pippin, you can do my routine work for the next two weeks, and keep your nose out of anything else. I don't want your help – not that a turnip-head like you could help a fellow like me. Don't you come mewling to me with any of your silly ideas – I just don't want to hear them.'

He put away all the clues in a box and locked it. 'Now I'm going along to interview the manager of the Little Theatre,' he said. 'Oh yes, I know *you've* interviewed him already Mr Clever – but I don't care what you've got out of him – it won't be anything worthwhile. Well, you get down to that writing I ticked you off about – and just remember this – I shan't forget your insubordination this morning over that there pestiferous dog. Yes, real insubordination – refusal to perform your rightful duties when commanded. Gah!'

Mr Goon made a dignified and haughty departure, walking ponderously down the path to his front gate, and shutting it sharply. Fatty, Buster, and Pippin were left together in the little sitting-room. Fatty put Buster down. He at once ran to Pippin and pawed eagerly at his legs, whining.

Pippin stooped down and patted him. He looked so miserable that Fatty wanted to comfort him.

'He's thanking you for sticking up for him,' he said. 'Thanks from me too, Mr Pippin. Awfully decent of you.'

'He's a nice dog,' said Pippin. 'I like dogs. I've got one of my own, back home. Mr Goon wouldn't let me bring him here.'

'I bet you think just about the same of Mr Goon

as I do – as we all do,' said Fatty. 'He's a beast. Always has been. He'd no right to speak to you in that way, you know.'

'I thought I was on to such a good case,' said Pippin, sitting down and taking out his fountain pen to write. 'I was going to send for Mr Goon this morning, of course – but he saw a notice in the paper and came tearing back, accusing me of not having told him anything. Now I've had to give him all my clues – and he'll use them instead of me.'

Fatty considered things carefully. Should he confess to PC Pippin now that they were not real clues? No – Mr Goon had them – let him mess about with them! Fatty thought that possibly PC Pippin might feel he ought to tell Mr Goon they were false clues, if he, Fatty, confessed to him that they were – and that would spoil everything. Mr Goon would go and complain to their parents, they would be forbidden to try and solve this mystery, and PC Pippin would be hauled over the coals by Mr Goon for being so stupid as to be taken in by false clues.

It would be very nice indeed if Mr Goon would busy himself with those clues, and leave the way clear for Fatty and the other Find-Outers to go to work! PC Pippin might help them. That would be better still.

'Mr Pippin, don't take any notice of what Mr Goon says to you,' said Fatty, earnestly. 'I am sure that Inspector Jenks, who is a great friend of ours, wouldn't allow him to speak to you like that, if he knew.'

'The Inspector told me about you and the others,' said Pippin. 'He's got a very high opinion of you, I must say. Said you'd been no end of a help in solving all kinds of mysterious cases.'

Fatty saw his chance and took it. 'Yes – that's true – and, Mr Pippin, I shall be on to this case too – and probably solve it! I should be very proud if you would help us – it would be nice to present the Inspector with another mystery correctly solved. He'd be thrilled.'

Pippin looked up at the earnest Fatty. Fatty was only a boy in his teens, but there was something about him that made people respect him and trust him. Brains? Yes. Character? Plenty! Cheek? Too much. Pluck? Any amount. Pippin saw all this as he looked at Fatty and sized him up. Well – if Inspector

Jenks liked this boy and admired him, then he, Pippin, was quite prepared to do the same – very willing to, in fact, seeing that it looked as if Fatty was not going to work with Mr Goon! Pippin couldn't help thinking it would be very nice indeed to help this boy to solve the mystery – what a blow for Mr Goon that would be!

'Well,' he said, and paused. 'Well – I'd like to help you – but wouldn't I have to tell Mr Goon anything we discovered?'

'But, Mr Pippin, didn't you hear him tell you that he didn't want your help?' said Fatty. 'Didn't you hear him say you weren't to go to him with any of your silly mewling ideas – whatever *they* are! You'd be disobeying his orders if you told him anything.'

This seemed a very sensible way out to Pippin. Yes – he certainly would be disobeying orders if he went and told Mr Goon anything now. On the other hand, surely it was his duty to work on the case if he could. Wasn't he the one to discover the robbery?

'I'll help you,' he told Fatty, and the boy grinned with pleasure. 'I guess if the Inspector has let you meddle in other cases, he'd say you could meddle in this one too. Anyway – I'd like to pay Goon back for some of the beastly things he said to me.'

'Hear, hear – very human and natural of you,' said Fatty, agreeing heartily. 'Well now, Mr Pippin, I'll lay my cards on the table – and you can lay yours there as well. I'll tell you all I know, and you can tell me all *you* know.'

'What do *you* know?' said Pippin, curiously.

'Well – I and the other four were round the back of the Little Theatre from about half past five last night till seven,' said Fatty. 'Just snooping about you know – looking at the posters and things.'

'Oh, you were, were you?' said Pippin, sitting up and taking notice. 'Did you see anything interesting?'

'I looked in at the window at the back of that verandah,' said Fatty. 'And I saw the pantomime cat there – at least, I feel sure that's what it must have been. It was like a huge furry cat. It came to the window and stared at me – gave me an awful scare. I saw it in the reflected light of the street lamp. Then, when Larry and Pip and I looked in later, we saw it sitting by the fire, pretending to wash itself like cats do. It waved its paw at us.'

Pippin was listening very earnestly indeed. 'This

is most interesting,' he said. 'You know – there doesn't appear to have been anyone at all in the Little Theatre when the robbery was committed – except the pantomime cat! Mr Goon wants to arrest him. He's sure he doped the manager and robbed the safe. Would you believe it – the pantomime cat!'

8. PIPPIN'S STORY – AND A MEETING

Fatty's brains began to work at top speed. 'Go on,' he said. 'Tell me all you know. What time were you there, Mr Pippin – what did you see – how did you discover the robbery and everything? My goodness, how lucky you were to be on the spot!'

'Well, actually I was after two rogues I'd seen under a bush the other night,' said Pippin, and Fatty had the grace to blush, though Pippin didn't notice it. 'I thought they might be meeting at the back of the Little Theatre, and I was hiding there. I got there at half past eight, and when I looked into the room at the back of the verandah – where you saw the cat – I saw him too. He was lying fast asleep by the fire. Funny to wear a cat-skin so long, isn't it?'

'Yes. Must be an odd fellow,' said Fatty.

'Well – he *is* odd – odd in the head,' said Pippin. 'I saw him this morning, without his cat-skin. He's not very big, except for his head. He's about twenty-four, they say, but he's never grown up really. Like a child the way he walks and acts. They call him Boysie.'

'I suppose he got dropped when he was a baby,' said Fatty, remembering stories he had heard. 'Babies like that don't develop properly, do they? Go on, Mr Pippin. This is thrilling.'

'Well, I saw the cat asleep by the fire as I said,' went on Pippin. 'Then, when the clock struck nine, I reckoned I'd better hide myself. So I climbed up through a hole in the verandah roof and sat on the windowsill of the room above, waiting. And I heard groans.'

'Go on,' said Fatty, as Pippin paused, remembering. 'Gosh, weren't you lucky to be there!'

'Well, I shone my torch into the room and saw the manager lying stretched out on his desk, and the empty safe in the wall behind him,' said Pippin. 'And I smashed the window and got in. The manager was already coming round. He was doped with some drug. I reckon it had been put into his cup of tea. The safe was quite empty, of course. It's being examined for fingerprints – I got an expert on the job at once – and the cup is being examined for drugs – just a strong sleeping-draught, I expect.'

'Who brought the manager the cup of tea – did he say?' asked Fatty, with interest.

'Yes – the pantomime cat!' said Pippin. 'Seems pretty suspicious, doesn't it? But if you talk to Boysie – the cat – you can't help thinking he'd got nothing to do with the whole thing – he's too silly – he wouldn't have the brains to put a sleeping-draught into a cup of tea, and he certainly wouldn't know where the safe was – or where to get the key – or how to find out the combination of letters that opens the safe door, once the key is in.'

'It's very interesting,' said Fatty. 'Who was in the Little Theatre at the time, besides Boysie?'

'Nobody,' said Pippin. 'Not a soul! All the cast – the actors and actresses, you know – had gone off after the free show they'd given to the children of the Farleigh Homes, and we can check their alibis – find out exactly where they were between the time of their leaving and eight o'clock. The deed was done between half past five and eight – between the time the show was over and the time the manager had drunk his cup of tea, and fallen unconscious.'

'I see. And you've got to check the whereabouts

of all the people who might have gone back and done the robbery,' said Fatty. 'Yes. But what's to prevent a stranger doing it – I mean, why should it be one of the actors?'

'Because whoever did it knew the best time to do it,' said Pippin. 'He knew where the safe was. He knew that the manager had put the takings there the day before and hadn't taken them to the bank that day, as he usually did. He knew where the key was kept – in the manager's wallet, not on his keyring – and he knew that the manager liked a cup of tea in the evening – and into it went the sleeping-draught!'

'Yes – you're right. No stranger would have known all those facts,' said Fatty, thoughtfully. 'It must be one of the cast – either an actor or an actress. It's strange that Boysie took in the tea, though, isn't it? Do you think he helped in the robbery?'

'I don't know! He says he doesn't remember a thing except feeling very sleepy last night and going to sleep in front of the fire,' said Pippin. 'That's certainly where *I* saw him when I looked into the room. He even said that he didn't take in the cup of tea to the manager, but that's nonsense, of course – the manager says he certainly did, and he wouldn't be likely to be mistaken. I think Boysie is scared, and said he didn't take in the tea to try and clear himself – forgetting he is quite unmistakeable as the pantomime cat!'

'Yes – it looks as if Boysie either did the whole thing or helped somebody else,' said Fatty. 'Well, thanks very much, Mr Pippin. I'll let you know if we spot anything. And remember – don't give anything away to Mr Goon. He won't thank you for it!'

'I shan't open my mouth to him,' said Pippin. 'My goodness – here he is, back again – and I haven't even begun this report he wants! You'd better clear out the back way, Frederick.'

Goon loomed up at the front gate, looking most important. He was talking to the vicar, solemnly and ponderously.

Fatty tiptoed out into the hall and made for the kitchen, with Buster in his arms. He meant to go into the back garden, hop over the fence at the bottom and make his way to Pip's. What a lot he had to tell the others!

He heard Mr Goon's loud voice. 'Do you know what the vicar tells me, Pippin? He tells me you were rude to his brother yesterday – snatched at his hat or something! Now, I really do think . . .'

But what Goon really did think Fatty didn't wait to hear. Poor PC Pippin! He was going to get into trouble over his curiosity about redheaded people now! Fatty couldn't help feeling very, very sorry!

If we'd known Mr Pippin was so decent we'd never have thought up all those tricks, said Fatty to himself, as he made his way to Pip's, where he knew the others would be anxiously awaiting him. Still – I can make it up to him, perhaps, by solving this peculiar mystery. The Mystery of the Pantomime Cat. Sounds good!

Larry, Daisy, Pip, and Bets had become very impatient indeed, waiting ages for Fatty. He had been gone for an hour and a half! What in the world could he be doing?

'Here he is at last,' called Bets from the window. 'Rushing up the drive with Buster. He looks full of importance – bursting with it. He must have plenty of news!'

He had. He began to relate everything from the

very beginning, and when he got to where Mr Goon had threatened Buster with a poker, Bets gave a scream, and flung herself down on the floor beside the surprised Scottie.

'Buster! Oh, Buster, how *could* anyone treat you like that! I hate Mr Goon! I do, I do. I know it's wrong to hate people, but it's worse *not* to hate cruel people like Mr Goon.'

Buster lay down on his tummy, wagging his plumy tail with pleasure at all this loving fuss. In fact, he was so thrilled that he hung his red tongue out and began to pant with joy.

'I wouldn't be a bit surprised if Bets took a poker to Mr Goon if she thought he was going to hurt Buster,' said Fatty. 'She may be frightened of him herself – but she'd be all pluck and no fright if she thought he was going to hurt anyone else! I know Bets!'

Bets was so pleased at this speech from Fatty. She went red and buried her face in Buster's neck. Fatty patted her on the back.

'I felt like banging Mr Goon on the head myself when I twisted the poker out of his hand,' he said. 'Oh my goodness – you should have seen his face when he found that I had the poker and he hadn't!'

'Go on with the story now,' said Pip. 'It's getting more and more exciting. Gosh, I wish I'd been there.'

Fatty went on with his tale. The children squealed with laughter when they heard that Mr Goon had demanded all the false clues, and had been solemnly handed them by PC Pippin.

'He'll meet that Sunday train. Fatty!' chuckled Pip, 'can't we meet it too?'

'Oh *yes*,' begged Bets. 'Let's. Do let's. Mr Goon would be awfully annoyed to see us all there. He'd think we knew the clue too.'

'Which we do,' said Larry. 'Seeing that we thought of it!'

'Yes – it's an idea,' said Fatty. 'Quite an idea. I've a good mind to disguise myself and arrive on that train – and arouse Mr Goon's suspicions and get him to follow me.'

'We could all follow too,' suggested Bets. 'We really must do that. It's tomorrow, isn't it? Oh Fatty, wouldn't it be fun?'

'Go on with the tale,' said Daisy. 'Let's hear it to the end before we make any more plans. It'll be dinnertime before Fatty's finished.'

Fatty then told the rest of the tale to the end. The children were very glad to hear that PC Pippin had stuck up for Buster and Fatty. They all agreed that PC Pippin was very nice indeed. They were thrilled to hear about the pantomime cat, and the two girls wished they had been brave enough to peep into the verandah room and see him the night before.

'Do you think he did it all?' asked Bets. 'If he took in the tea, he must have done it. He may be cleverer than we think.'

'He may be, Bets,' said Fatty. 'I shall have to interview him. In fact, I thought we all could – together, you know, just as if we were children interested in him. He may be on his guard with grown-ups. He wouldn't be with children.'

'Yes. That's a good idea,' said Larry. 'Gosh, what a thrill this is! To think we put our clues in the very place where all this was going to happen – and managed to put a policeman there too, so that he would discover the crime. It's extraordinary.'

'Well – we must set our wits to work,' said Fatty. 'We've only got just over two weeks to solve the mystery – and Mr Goon is on the job too – hampered by a few false clues, of course! But we've got PC Pippin to help us. He may learn a few things that it's impossible for us to find out.'

'How are we going to set to work?' asked Larry.

'We must make a plan,' said Fatty. 'A properly set-out plan. Like we usually do. List of suspects, list of clues, and so on.'

'Oooh yes,' said Bets. 'Let's begin now, Fatty. This very minute. Have you got a notebook?'

'Of course,' said Fatty, and took out a fat notebook and a very fine pen. He ruled a few lines very neatly. 'Now then – SUSPECTS.'

A call came from the hall. Bets groaned. 'Blow! Dinner already! Fatty, will you come this afternoon and do it?'

'Right,' said Fatty, 'Half past two everyone – and put your best thinking-caps on! This is the finest mystery we've had yet!'

9. PIPPIN IS A HELP

Fatty thought hard during his lunch. His mother found him very silent indeed, and began to wonder about his teeth again. She looked at him closely. His cheeks seemed to have subsided – they were not very swollen now!

'Frederick – how is your tooth?' she asked suddenly.

Fatty looked at his mother blankly. His tooth? What did she mean?

'My tooth?' he said. 'What tooth, Mummy?'

'Now don't be silly, Frederick,' said his mother. 'You know how swollen your face was this morning. I meant to ring the dentist but I forgot. I was just asking you how your tooth was – it must have been bad because you had such a swollen face. I think I'd better ring up the dentist, even though your face *has* gone down.'

'Mummy,' said Fatty desperately, 'that wasn't

toothache – it was cheek-pads.'

Now it was his mother's turn to look at him blankly. 'Cheek-pads! What *do* you mean, Frederick?'

'Things you put in your cheeks to alter your appearance,' explained Fatty, wishing heartily that he had not tried them out on his mother. 'A – a sort of disguise.'

'How very disgusting,' said his mother. 'I do wish you wouldn't do things like that, Frederick. No wonder you looked so awful.'

'Sorry Mummy,' said Fatty, hoping she would talk about something else. She did. She talked about the extraordinary behaviour of Mr Pippin who had snatched at Mr Twit's hair, or hat, she didn't know which. And she also told Fatty that the vicar had complained about it to Mr Goon, now that he was back again to take charge of this new robbery case at the Little Theatre.

'And I do hope, Frederick,' said his mother, 'I *do* hope you won't try and meddle in *this* case. Apparently Mr Goon is well on the way to finding out everything, and has a most remarkable collection of clues. I do *not* like that man, but he certainly seems to have been very quick off the mark in this case – came straight back from his holiday, found all these clues, and is on the track of the robber at once!'

'Don't you believe it,' murmured Fatty, half under his breath.

'What did you say, Frederick? I wish you wouldn't mumble,' said his mother. 'Well, I don't suppose you know a thing about this case, so just keep out of it and don't annoy Mr Goon.'

Fatty didn't answer. He knew a lot about the case, and he meant to meddle in it, for all he was worth, and if he could annoy Mr Goon, he was certainly going to. But he couldn't possibly tell his mother all that! So he sank into silence once more and began to think hard about all the suspects.

He would have to find out their names and who they were and where they lived. It was pretty obvious that only one of the theatre people could have committed the crime. One of them had come back that night, let himself in quietly, and done the deed. But which one?

Fatty decided he must go to Mr Pippin and get the list of names and addresses. He would do that immediately after his lunch. So, at a quarter to two, when he left the table, Fatty rushed off to see if Mr Pippin was available. If Mr Goon was at home, it was no good. He couldn't possibly ask PC Pippin anything in front of Mr Goon.

He walked by the sitting-room window of the little cottage belonging to Mr Goon. Pippin was there, facing the window. Goon was also there, his back to it, writing at the table. Fatty tiptoed to the window and tried to attract Pippin's attention. Pippin looked up, astonished to see Fatty winking and beckoning outside. He turned round cautiously to see what Mr Goon was doing.

When he turned back again he saw, held up to the window, a piece of paper on which Fatty had written,

MEET ME IN HIGH STREET TEN MINUTES' TIME.

Pippin grinned and nodded. Fatty disappeared. Goon heard the click of the gate and turned round.

'Who's that coming in?' said Goon.

'No one,' said Pippin, truthfully.

'Well, who was it going out then?' said Goon.

'Can't see anyone,' said Pippin.

'Gah! Call yourself a policeman and you can't see who opens a gate in front of your nose,' said Goon, who had eaten too much lunch and was feeling very bad-tempered. Pippin said nothing at all. He was getting used to Mr Goon's remarks.

He finished what he was doing and then got up. 'Where are you going?' asked Goon.

'Out to the post office,' said Pippin. 'I'm off duty at the moment, Mr Goon, as you very well know. If there's anything wants doing, I'll do it when I come back.'

And in spite of Goon's snort, Pippin walked out of the house and up to the post office. He posted his letter and then looked for Fatty. Ah, there he was, sitting on the wooden bench. Pippin went up to him. They grinned at one another and Buster rubbed against Pippin's trousers.

'Come into that shop over there and have a lemonade,' said Fatty. 'I don't want Mr Goon to see us hob-nobbing together.'

They went into the little shop, sat down, and Fatty ordered lemonades. Then, in a low voice,

Fatty told Pippin what he wanted.

'Do you know the names and addresses of the actors and actresses at the Little Theatre?' he asked.

'Yes,' said Pippin, at once. 'I got them all last night. Wait a bit – I think they're in my notebook. I don't believe I gave them to Mr Goon. He's been out interviewing the whole lot, and I expect he got the names from the manager – same as I did.'

'Oh – he's interviewed them already, has he?' said Fatty. 'He can get going when he likes, can't he?'

'Yes,' said Pippin. 'He's found one of them has a name beginning with Z too – you know one of the clues was an old handkerchief with Z on it. Well, see here,' and he pointed to one of the names in the list he was now showing to Fatty, 'the name of Dick Whittington, the principal boy – who's acted by a girl – is Zoe Markham. Looks as if Zoe was out on that verandah for some reason or other – at a meeting of the crooks, perhaps.'

Fatty was horror-stricken. To think that there was actually somebody with a name beginning with Z! Who would have thought it? He didn't know what to say. At all costs, he would have to clear Zoe somehow. Fatty wished very heartily for the hundredth time that he and the others hadn't started PC Pippin on a false mystery complete with false clues.

'Has Zoe got an alibi – someone to swear that she was somewhere else between half past five and eight o'clock?' asked Fatty, looking worried.

'Oh yes. They've all got alibis,' said Pippin. 'Every one of them. I interviewed them myself last night, the whole lot – and Mr Goon gave them the once-over again this morning. Alibis all correct.'

'Mysterious, isn't it?' said Fatty, after a silence. 'I mean – it *must* be one of those theatre people, mustn't it? Nobody else had so much inside knowledge as to be able to give the manager a cup of tea, and then take down the mirror, find the key, work out the combination, and open the safe.'

'Don't forget it was the pantomime cat who took in the cup of tea,' said Pippin.

'Yes. That's stranger still,' said Fatty. 'Anyone would think he'd done the job.'

'Mr Goon thinks so,' said Pippin. 'He thinks all that business of the cat saying he doesn't understand, and he doesn't remember, and bursting into tears is put on – good acting, you know.'

'What do *you* think?' asked Fatty. Pippin considered. 'I told you before. I think Boysie's a bit funny in the head – never grown up, poor fellow. You know, I've got a cousin like that – and he wouldn't hurt a fly. It's a fact, he wouldn't. I don't see how he could possibly have done all that. I'm sorry Mr Goon's got it into his head that Boysie's done the job – he'll scare the poor chap into fits.'

'Well – it's quite possible that somebody hid in the kitchen somewhere when Boysie was making the tea, and popped something into the cup when Boysie wasn't looking,' said Fatty.

'Yes. There's something in that,' said Pippin. 'But we still come back to the fact that it can only have been done by one of the theatre folk – no one else knows enough to have done it – and they all have alibis – so there you are!'

'Can I have their names and addresses?' asked Fatty. 'I'll copy them down.' Pippin handed over his notebook. Fatty looked through the pages with interest. 'Gosh – are these your notes about where they said they were between half past five and eight o'clock last night?'

'That's right,' said Pippin. 'Take them along with you, if you like. Save you a lot of trouble! They've all been interviewed twice, so you can take my word for it they won't say anything different the third time – that's if you were thinking of interviewing them, Frederick.'

'We're making out a plan,' said Fatty, stuffing the notes into his pocket. 'I don't quite know what it will be yet. I'll tell you when we know details. Thanks very much, Mr Pippin.'

'If you ever see a villainous-looking tramp with red hair, let me know, will you?' said Pippin. 'I mean – you get about a lot on that bike of yours – and you might happen on the fellow – and his mate with him. The ones I saw under the bush that night in Willow Road, I mean.'

'Er – yes – I know the ones you mean,' said Fatty, feeling extremely guilty at this mention of the red-haired villain. 'I'll certainly let you know if I see him again. But I don't think he had anything to do with this robbery job, you know.'

'Ah, you can't tell,' said Pippin, finishing his glass

of lemonade and standing up. 'If ever I saw wickedness in anyone's face, it was in that red-haired fellow's. I wouldn't care to be seen in *his* company. I'll walk a little way with you, Frederick – it's a nice day. Your dog all right?'

'Yes thanks,' said Fatty. 'Takes a lot to upset a Scottie like Buster!'

'That properly turned me against Mr Goon, that did,' said Pippin, as they walked down the High Street – and round the corner they bumped straight into Mr Goon! He glared at them both, and Buster flew round him delightedly.

'Buster, come here,' ordered Fatty, in such a stern voice that Buster felt he had to obey. He put his tail down and crept behind Fatty, keeping up a continuous growl.

'You be careful of the company you keep, Pippin,' ordered Mr Goon. 'I warned you against that boy, didn't I? Always interfering and meddling, he is! Anyway, he can't interfere in *this* case much! Cast-iron, that's what it is! I'll be making an arrest any time now!'

Mr Goon walked on, and Pippin and Fatty looked at one another with raised eyebrows.

'It's that pantomime cat he's going to arrest,' said Pippin. 'I saw it in his eyes! And before he's finished with that poor cat he'll make him confess to things he didn't do. He will!'

'Then I'll have to see that he doesn't,' said Fatty. 'I must set the old brains to work IMMEDIATELY!'

10. THE SUSPECTS AND THEIR ALIBIS

At just half past two, Fatty walked into Pip's drive for the second time that day, and was hailed by Bets from the open window.

'Hurry up, Fatty! We want to make our plan!'

Fatty hurried, grinning at Bets' impatience. He went up the stairs two at a time, and found the other four waiting for him round the table.

'Ha! A conference!' said Fatty. 'Well – I've got some information here which we'll study together. Then we'll really get going.'

He told the children quickly what PC Pippin had told him, and then got out the notebook with names, addresses and particulars of alibis in. The word 'alibi' was new to Bets, and had to be explained to her.

'Is it anything to do with lullaby?' she asked, and the others roared.

'No, Bets,' said Fatty. 'I'll tell you what an alibi is.

Suppose somebody smashed this window, and your mother thought it was Pip – and Pip told her he was with me at the time, and I said yes, he certainly was – then I am Pip's *alibi* – he's got his alibi, because I can vouch for his being with me when the window was smashed.'

'I see,' said Bets. 'And if somebody said that at just this moment you had hit Mr Goon on the head, and we said no, you couldn't have, because you were with us – we'd *all* be alibis for you.'

'Quite right, Bets – you've got the idea,' grinned Fatty. 'Well – I've got a list of the alibis of all the suspects here – which will be very, very useful. Listen and I'll read out the names of the suspects first, and then I'll tell you their alibis and what we know about them.'

He read from PC Pippin's notes.

SUSPECTS

Number one. Pantomime Cat, *otherwise known as Boysie Summers. Was in theatre at the time in question. Took manager a cup of tea before eight o'clock. Says he didn't, but admits he had a cup of tea himself. Says he went to sleep most of the evening.*

Number two. Zoe Markham, *who plays the part of Dick Whittington. Says she left theatre with other members of the cast, and went to her sister's, where she played with the children and helped to put them to bed. Her sister is Mrs Thomas, and she lives at Green House, Hemel Road.*

'I know her!' said Daisy. 'She's awfully nice. She's got two dear little children. One's having a birthday soon, I know.'

'Hey,' said Larry suddenly. '*Zoe* Markham! I hope Mr Goon doesn't connect up the Z for Zoe with the Z on that old hanky of Daisy's – the one we used for a false clue.'

'I rather think he has,' said Fatty. 'We'll have to do something about that, if so. Well – to continue . . .'

Number three. Lucy White, *who plays the part of Margot, Dick Whittington's sweetheart. Says she went to call on Miss Adams, an old*

*age pensioner who is ill, at address 11 Mark
Street. Sat with her till nine o'clock, and
helped her with her knitting.*

'Miss Adams is a friend of our cook's,' said Larry.
'She used to come and help with the sewing.
Nice lady.'

*Number four. Peter Watting, who plays the
part of Dick's master. Elderly, and rather
obstructive. Would not answer questions readily.
Said he was out walking with suspect number
five at the time.*

*Number five. William Orr, who plays the part
of the captain of Dick's ship. Young man, affable
and helpful. Says he was out walking with Peter
Watting at the time.*

'Then those two are alibis for each other,' said Larry,
with interest. 'What's to stop them from *both* going
back to the theatre and doing the robbery, and then
giving each other an alibi?'

'That's a good point, Larry,' said Fatty. 'Very good

point. PC Pippin doesn't seem to have worked that out. Wait a bit – here's another note about it. "Suspects four and five (Peter Watting and William Orr) further said they had gone for a walk by the river, and had called at a teashop called "The Turret" for some sandwiches and coffee. They did not know the exact time".'

'Bit fishy, I think,' said Pip. 'Wants looking into.'

> *Number six.* Alec Grant, *who plays the part of Dick's mother. Usually takes women's parts and is very good at them, a fine mimic and good actor. Says he was giving a show at Hetton Hall, Sheepridge, that evening, from six to ten – acting various women's parts to an audience of about one hundred.*

'Well! That rules *him* out!' said Larry. 'He's got a hundred alibis, not one.'

'Yes. It certainly clears *him*,' said Fatty. 'Well, here's the last suspect.'

> *Number seven.* John James, *who plays the part of the king in the play. Says he went to*

the cinema and was there all the evening,
seeing the film called, You Know How It Is.

'Not much of an alibi either,' said Pip. 'He could easily have popped in, and popped out again – and even popped back in again after doing the robbery. Poor alibi, I call that.'

'Well now,' said Fatty, 'I imagine that Mr Goon will check all these, if he hasn't already – but he's such a mutt that I expect he'll miss something important that *we* might spot. So I vote we all check up on the various alibis ourselves.'

There was a deep silence. Nobody felt capable of doing this. It was bad enough to interview people – it was much worse to check an alibi!

'I can't,' said Bets, at last. 'I know I'm a Find-Outer and I ought to do what you tell me, Fatty, but I really *can't* check an ali–alibi. I mean – it sounds too much like a *real* detective.'

'Well, we may be kids, but we're really good detectives all the same,' said Fatty. 'Look at all the mysteries we've solved already! This is a bit more *advanced*, perhaps.'

'It's very advanced,' groaned Larry. 'I feel rather

'like Bets – out of my depth.'

'Don't give up before you've begun,' said Fatty. 'Now, I'll tell you what I propose to do.'

'What?' asked everyone, and Buster thumped his tail on the ground as if he too had a great interest in the question.

'There are three things we must do,' said Fatty. 'We must interview Boysie, and see what *we* think of him – and we'll interview him all together, as we suggested before.'

'Right,' said Larry. 'What next?'

'We'll see every other suspect too,' said Fatty.

There was a general groan.

'Oh *no*, Fatty – six people! And all grown up! We can't possibly,' said Daisy. 'What excuse could we have for seeing them even?'

'A very good excuse indeed,' said Fatty. 'All we've got to do is to find our autograph books and go and ask for autographs – and we can easily say a few words to them then, can't we?'

'That's a *brilliant* idea,' said Pip. 'Really brilliant, Fatty. I must say you think of good ideas.'

'Oh well,' said Fatty, modestly, 'I've got a few brains, you know. As a matter-of-fact . . .'

'*Don't* start telling us about the wonderful things you did at school last term,' begged Pip. 'Go on with our plan.'

'All right,' said Fatty, a little huffily. 'The third thing we must do is, as I said, check up on the alibis – and if we think hard, it won't be so difficult. For instance, Daisy says she knows Zoe Markham's sister, who lives near her, and she also says one of the children is having a birthday soon. Well Daisy, what's to stop you and Bets from taking the child a present, getting into conversation with the mother, and finding out if Zoe *was* there all that evening? Zoe's sister wouldn't be on her guard with two children who came with a present for her child.'

'Yes – all right, Fatty, I can do that,' said Daisy. 'You'll come too, won't you Bets?'

'Yes,' said Bets. 'But you'll ask the questions, won't you Daisy?'

'You've got to help,' said Daisy. 'I'm not doing it all!'

'Now, the next suspect is Lucy White who went to sit with Miss Adams, an old age pensioner,' went on Fatty. 'Larry, you said she was a friend of your cook's, and used to come to help with the sewing.

Can't you and Daisy concoct some sort of sewing job you want done, and take it round to her – and ask a few questions about Lucy White?'

'Yes, we could,' said Daisy. 'I'll pretend I want to give Mother a surprise for Easter, and I'll take round a cushion cover I want embroidering, or something. I've been there before, and Mary Adams knows me.'

'Splendid,' said Fatty. 'That's two alibis we can check very easily indeed. Now, the next one – well, the next two, actually, because they are each other's alibis – Peter Watting and William Orr. Well, they apparently went to a place called "The Turret" and had coffee and sandwiches there. Pip, you and I will call there and also have coffee and sandwiches tomorrow morning.'

'But it's Sunday and I have to go to church,' objected Pip.

'Oh yes. I forgot it was Sunday,' said Fatty. 'Well, we'll do that on Monday or Tuesday morning. Now, suspect number six is Alec Grant, who was apparently giving a concert at Hetton Hall to about a hundred people. Seems hardly necessary to check that.'

'Well, don't let's,' said Larry.

'The thing is – a really good detective always checks *every*thing,' said Fatty. 'Even if he thinks it really isn't necessary. So I suppose we'd better check that too. Bets, you can come with me and check it. We'll find someone who attended the show, and ask them about it and see if Alec Grant really was there.'

'Right,' said Bets, who never minded what she did with Fatty. She always felt so safe with him, as safe as if she was with a grown-up.

'That only leaves one more,' said Fatty, looking at his list. 'And that's John James who says he went to the cinema all evening.

'Yes – and we thought it was a pretty poor alibi,' said Pip. 'Who's going to check that one up?'

'Oh – Larry and I could tackle that, I think, or you and Larry,' said Fatty.

'But how?' asked Larry.

'Have to think of something,' said Fatty. 'Well, there you are, Find-Outers – plenty for us to find out! We've got to see Boysie, got to get autographs from all the cast and have a look at them – and got to check up on all the alibis. Pretty stiff work.'

'*And*, Fatty, we've got to meet that train

tomorrow and lead old Mr Goon a dance,' Bets reminded him. 'Don't let's forget that!'

'Oh no – we really must do that,' grinned Fatty. 'I'll use my new cheek-pads for that.'

'Whatever are those?' said Bets in wonder, and screamed with laughter when Fatty told her. 'Oh yes, do wear those. I hope I don't giggle when I see you.'

'You'd better not, young Bets,' said Fatty, getting hold of her nose and pulling it gently. 'Now what time's that train we underlined?'

'Half past three tomorrow afternoon,' said Pip. 'We'll all be there, Fatty. What will *you* do – go to the next station, catch the train there, and arrive here at half past three?'

'I will,' said Fatty. 'Look out for me. So long, everyone. I've just remembered that my mother told me to be home an hour ago, to meet my great-aunt. *What* a memory I've got!'

11. TREAT FOR MR GOON

Fatty worked out the timetable for putting the plan into action that evening. They couldn't do much the next day, Sunday, that was certain. Daisy had better buy a present for Zoe's sister's child on Monday and take it in with Bets. The next day, perhaps she and Larry could go and see Miss Adams and find out about Lucy White.

He and Larry would go to 'The Turret' on Monday and have coffee and sandwiches and see if they could find out anything about Peter Watting and William Orr. They could leave Alec Grant till last, because it really did seem as if his alibi was unshakable, as it consisted of about a hundred people. He would not dare to give an alibi like that if it were not true.

I can't think how to find out about the last fellow's alibi – what's his name? – John James, said Fatty to himself. Can't very well go and talk to a cinema and ask it questions! Still, I'll think of something.

He paused and looked at himself in the mirror. He was thinking out his disguise for the next day – something perfectly reasonable, but peculiar, and with red hair so that it would attract Mr Goon's attention. He would wear dark glasses and pretend to be short-sighted. That would make the children want to laugh.

We'll go and see Boysie – what a name – on Monday morning, thought Fatty, drawing a line round both his nostrils to see what effect it gave.

Gracious! Don't I look bad-tempered! Grrrrr! Gah!

He removed the lines and experimented with different eyebrows, thinking of his plan the whole time.

We'll all go and ask for autographs after the afternoon performance at the Little Theatre on Monday, thought Fatty. And dear me – why shouldn't we *go* to the performance and see everyone in action? It mightn't tell us anything – but on the other hand, it might! That's a jolly good idea. Well – Monday's going to be pretty busy, I can see, what with interviewing and asking for autographs and checking up alibis. Now, what about that train tomorrow? Shall I speak to Mr Goon when I see him or not? I'll ask him the way somewhere!

He began to practise different voices. First, a deepdown rumble, modelled on a preacher who had come to his school to preach one Sunday, and who had been the admiration of everyone because of his extremely bass voice.

He tried a high falsetto voice – no, not so good. He tried a foreign voice – ah, that was splendid.

'Please, Sair, to teel me ze way to Hoffle-Foffle Road!' began Fatty. 'What you say, Sair? I not unnerstand. I say, I weesh to know ze way to Hoffle-Foffle Road. HOFFLE-FOFFLE!'

There came a knock at his door. 'Frederick. Have you got Pip and the others in there with you? You know I don't like them here so late at night.'

Fatty opened his door in surprise. 'Oh no, Mummy – of course they're not here. There's only me!'

His mother looked at him and made an exasperated noise. 'Frederick! What have you done to your eyebrows, they are all crooked! And what's that around your eye?'

'Oh – only a wrinkle I drew there for an experiment,' said Fatty, rubbing it away hastily. 'And you needn't worry about my eyebrows, Mummy. They're not really crooked. Look.'

He took off the eyebrows he was wearing, and showed his mother his own underneath. They were not at all crooked, of course!

'Well, what will you think of next Frederick?' said his mother, half-crossly. 'I came to say that Daddy wants you to listen to the next bit on the radio with him – it's about a part of China he knows very well. Are you *sure* you haven't got anyone else with you here? I did hear quite a lot of voices when I was coming up the stairs.'

'Mummy, look under the bed, behind the curtains and in the cupboard,' said Fatty generously. But she wouldn't, of course, and proceeded downstairs – but stopped in a hurry when she heard a falsetto voice say, 'Has she gone? Can I come out?'

She turned at once, annoyed to think there was someone in Fatty's room after all – but when she saw Fatty's grinning face, she laughed too.

'Oh – one of your voices, I suppose,' she sa
might have guessed. I cannot think, Frederick, how
it is that you always have such good reports from
school. I cannot believe you behave well there.'

'Well, Mummy,' said Fatty, in his most modest
voice, 'the fact is, brains *will* tell, you know. I can't
help having good brains, can I? I mean . . .'

'Shh!' said his father, as they walked into the
sitting-room. 'The talk's begun.'

So it had – and a very dull talk it proved to be,
on a little-known part of China which Fatty
devoutly hoped he would never have to visit. He
passed the dull half hour by thinking out further
plans. His father was really pleased to see such an
intent look on Fatty's face.

The Find-Outers were finding the time very
long, as they always did when something exciting
was due to happen. Bets could hardly wait for the
next afternoon to come. How would Fatty be
disguised? What would he say? Would he wink
at them?

At twenty-five past three, Larry, Daisy, Pip, and
Bets walked sedately onto the platform. A minute
later, Mr Goon arrived, a little out of breath,

because he had had an argument with PC Pippin, and had had to hurry. He saw the children at once and glared at them.

'What you here for?' he demanded.

'Same reason as you, I suppose,' said Pip. 'To meet someone.'

'We're meeting Fatty,' piped up Bets, and got a nudge from Larry.

'It's all right,' whispered Bets. 'I'm not giving anything away, really – he won't know it's Fatty when he sees him – you know he won't.'

The train came in with a clatter and stopped. Quite a lot of people got out. Mr Goon eyed them all carefully. He was standing by the platform door, leading to the booking-office, and everyone had to pass him to give up their tickets. The four children stood nearby, watching out for Fatty.

Bets nudged Pip. A voluminous old lady was proceeding down the platform, a veil spreading out behind her in the wind. Pip shook his head. No – good as Fatty was at disguises, he could never look like that imperious old lady.

A man came by, hobbling along with a stick, his hat pulled down over his eyes, and a shapeless mackintosh flung across his shoulders. He had a straggling moustache and an absurd little beard. His hair was a little reddish, and Mr Goon gave him a very sharp look indeed.

But Bets knew it wasn't Fatty. This man had a crooked nose, and Fatty surely couldn't mimic a thing like that.

It looked almost as if Goon was about to follow this man – and then he saw someone else – someone with much redder hair, someone much more suspicious.

This man was evidently a foreigner of some sort. He wore a peculiar hat on his red hair, which was neatly brushed. He had a foreign-looking cape round his shoulders, and brightly polished, pointed shoes.

For some peculiar reason, he wore bicycle clips round the bottoms of his trousers, and this made him even more foreign-looking, though Bets didn't quite know why it should. The man wore dark glasses on his nose, had a little red moustache, and his cheeks were very bulgy. He was very freckled indeed. Bets wondered admiringly how Fatty managed to produce freckles like that.

She knew it was Fatty, of course, and so did the others, though if they had not been actually looking for him, they would have been very doubtful indeed. But there was something about the jaunty way he walked and looked about that made them quite certain.

The foreigner brushed against Bets as he came to the exit. He dug his elbow into her, and she almost giggled.

'Your ticket, sir,' said the collector, as Fatty seemed to have forgotten all about this. Fatty began to feel in all his pockets, one after another, exclaiming in annoyance.

'This tick-ett! I had him, I know I had him! He was green.'

Mr Goon watched him intently, quite ready to arrest him if he didn't produce his ticket! The foreigner suddenly swooped down by Mr Goon's feet, and shoved one of them aside with his hand. Goon glared.

'Here. What are you doing?' he began.

'A million apologeeze,' said the stranger, waving his ticket in Goon's face, and almost scraping the skin off the end of the policeman's big nose. 'I have him – he was on the ground, and you put your beeg foots on him. Aha!'

Fatty thrust the ticket at the astonished collector, and pushed past Goon. Then he stopped so suddenly that Goon jumped.

'Ah, you are the pliss, are you not?' demanded Fatty, peering at Goon short-sightedly from his dark glasses. 'At first I think you are an engine-driver – but now I see you are the pliss.'

'Yes. I'm the police,' said Mr Goon gruffly, feeling more and more suspicious of this behaviour. 'Where do you want to go? I expect you're a stranger here.'

'Ah yes, alas! A strangair,' agreed Fatty. 'I need to know my way to a place. You will tell me zis place?'

'Certainly,' said Mr Goon, only too pleased.

'It is – er – it is – Hoffle-Foffle House, in Willow Road,' said Fatty, making a great to-do with the Hoffle-Foffle bit. Goon looked blank.

'No such place as – er – what you said,' he answered.

'I say Hoffle-Foffle – you say you do not know it? How can zis be?' cried Fatty, and walked out into the road at top speed with Mr Goon at his heels.

Fatty stopped abruptly and Mr Goon bumped into him. Bets by this time was so convulsed with laughter that she had to stay behind.

'There isn't a house of that name,' said Goon exasperated. 'Who do you want to see?'

'That ees my own business – vairy, vairy secret beeziness,' said Fatty. 'Where is zis Willow Road? I will find Hoffle-Foffle by myself.'

Goon directed him. Fatty set off at top speed again, and Mr Goon followed, panting. The four children followed too, trying to suppress their giggles. Hoffle-Foffle House was, of course, not to be found.

'I will sairch the town till I see zis place,' Fatty told Mr Goon earnestly. 'Do not accompany me, Mr Pliss – I am tired of you.'

Whereupon Fatty set off at a great pace again, and left Mr Goon behind. He saw the four children still following, and frowned. Little pests! Couldn't he shadow anyone without them coming too? 'Clear orf!' he said to them, as they came up. 'Do you hear me? Clear orf!'

'Can't we even go for a walk, Mr Goon?' said Daisy pathetically, and Mr Goon snorted and hastened to follow 'that dratted foreigner,' who by now was almost out of sight.

Mr Goon, in fact, almost lost him. Fatty was getting tired of this protracted walk, and wanted to throw Mr Goon off, and go home and laugh with the others. But Mr Goon valiantly pursued him. So Fatty made a pretence of examining the names of many houses, peering at them through his dark glasses. He was getting nearer and nearer to his own home by this time.

He managed to pop in at his front gate and scuttled down to the shed at the bottom of the garden, where he locked the door, and began to pull off his disguise as quickly as he could. He wiped his face free of paint, pulled off his false eyebrows and wig, took out his cheek-pads, straightened his tie, and ventured out into the garden.

He saw the four children looking anxiously over the fence. 'Mr Goon's gone in to tell your mother,' whispered Larry. 'He thinks the suspicious foreigner is somewhere in the garden and he wants permission to search for him.'

'Let him,' grinned Fatty. 'Oh my, how I want to laugh! Sh! Here's Mr Goon and Mummy.'

Fatty strolled up to meet them. 'Why, Mr Goon,' he began, 'what a pleasant surprise!'

'I thought those friends of yours had gone to meet you at the station,' said Mr Goon suspiciously.

'Quite right,' said Fatty politely. 'They did meet me. Here they are.'

The other four had gone in at the gate at the bottom of the garden, and were now trooping demurely up the garden path behind Fatty. Goon stared at them in surprise.

'But – they've been following *me* about all afternoon,' he began. 'And I certainly didn't see you at the station.'

'Oh, but Mr Goon, he *was* there,' said Larry, earnestly. 'Perhaps you didn't recognise him. He does look different sometimes, you know.'

'Mr Goon,' interrupted Mrs Trotteville, impatiently, 'you wanted to look for some suspicious trespasser in my garden. It's Sunday afternoon and I want to go back to my husband. Never mind about these children.'

'Yes, but,' began Mr Goon, trying to sort things out in his mind, and failing. How *could* these kids have met Fatty if he wasn't there? How dare they say they had met him, when he knew jolly well the four of them had been trailing him all that afternoon? There was something very peculiar here.

'Well, Mr Goon, I'll leave you,' said Mrs Trotteville. 'I've no doubt the children will help you look for your suspicious loiterer.'

She went in. The children began to look everywhere with such terrific enthusiasm that Mr Goon gave up. He was sure he'd never find that red-haired foreigner again. *Could* it have been Fatty in one of his disguises? No – not possible! Nobody would have the sauce to lead him on a wild-goosechase like that. And now he hadn't solved the mystery of who was coming by that half past three train! He snorted and went crossly out of the front gate.

The children flung themselves down on the damp ground and laughed till they cried. They laughed so much that they didn't see a very puzzled Mr Goon looking over the fence at them. *Now* what was the joke? Those dratted children! Slippery as eels they were – couldn't trust them an inch!

Mr Goon went back home, tired and cross.

'Interfering with the law!' he muttered, to PC Pippin's surprise. 'Always interfering with the law! One of these days, I'll catch them good and proper – and then they'll laugh on the other side of their faces. Gah!'

12. ZOE, THE FIRST SUSPECT

The next day, Monday, the Five Find-Outers really set to work. They all met at Pip's as usual. They were early, half past nine – but, as Fatty pointed out, they had a lot to do.

'You and Bets must go and buy a birthday present for that child – Zoe Markham's niece,' he said. 'Got any money?'

'I haven't any at all,' said Bets. 'I owe Pip for a water pistol, and it's all gone to pay for that.'

'I've got a little, I think,' said Daisy.

Fatty put his hand into his pocket and pulled out some silver. He always seemed to have plenty of money. He had aunts and uncles who treated him well, and he was just like a grown-up the way he always seemed to have enough to spend.

He picked out a few pound coins. 'Here you are, Daisy. You can get a little something with that. When's the child's birthday?'

'Tomorrow,' said Daisy, 'I met her little sister yesterday and asked her.'

'Good,' said Fatty. 'Couldn't be better! Now you go and buy something, you and Bets, and put a message on it, and deliver it to Mrs Thomas, Zoe's sister. And mind you get into conversation with her and find out exactly when Zoe went there on Friday night, and what time she left.'

'How shall we get her talking though?' said Daisy, beginning to feel nervous.

Fatty looked sternly at poor Daisy. 'Now I really can't plan everyone's conversation! It's up to you to get this done, Daisy. Use your common sense. Ask what the mum herself is giving the child – something like that – and I bet she'll take you in to see the present she's bought.'

'Oh yes – that's a good idea,' said Daisy, cheering up. 'Come on Bets – we'll go and do our bit of shopping.'

'I'm going to see PC Pippin for a few minutes, if I can,' said Fatty. 'I want to find out one or two things before I make further plans.'

'What do you want to know?' asked Larry, interested.

'Well – I want to know if there were any fingerprints on that wall-mirror, which had to be lifted down to get the safe open, at the back of it,' said Fatty. 'And there might have been prints on the safe too. If there were, and the job was done by one of the actors or actresses, we might as well give up our detecting at once – because Mr Goon has only got to take everyone's fingerprints, compare them with the ones on the mirror or safe – and there you are! He'd have the thief immediately!'

'Oh, I hope he won't!' said Bets, in dismay. 'I want to go on with this mystery. I want *us* to solve it, not Mr Goon. I like this finding-out part.'

'Don't worry,' said Fatty, with a grin. 'The thief wouldn't leave prints behind, I'm sure! He was pretty cunning, whoever he was.'

'Do you think it *was* Boysie, the pantomime cat?' asked Daisy.

'No – not at present, anyway,' said Fatty. 'Wait and see what we think of him when we see him. Oh, and Larry, will you and Pip go along to the theatre this morning and get tickets for this afternoon's show? Here's the money.'

And out came the handful of money again!

'It's a good thing you're so *rich*, Fatty,' said Bets. 'We wouldn't find detecting nearly as easy if you weren't!'

'Now, let's see,' said Fatty. 'We've all got jobs to do this morning, haven't we? Report back here at twelve, or as near that as possible. I'm off to see PC Pippin, if I can manage to get him alone. Come on, Buster. Wake up! Bicycle basket for you!'

Buster opened his eyes, got up from the hearth rug, yawned and wagged his tail. He trotted sedately after Fatty. Bets went to put on her coat, ready to do the bit of birthday shopping with Daisy. Pip and Larry went to get their bicycles, meaning to ride down to the Little Theatre to get the tickets.

Fatty was just wheeling his bicycle from Pip's shed. He called to the other two. 'Pip! Larry! Don't just buy the tickets – talk to as many people down there as you can! See if you can find out anything at all.'

'Right, Captain!' grinned Larry. 'We'll do our best.'

Off went all Five Find-Outers – and Dog – to do a really good morning's detection work. Bets and Daisy walked, as Bets' bike had a puncture.

They were soon down in the town, and went to the toy-shop there.

'Jane's only four,' said Daisy. 'She won't want anything too advanced. It's no good buying her a difficult game or puzzle. We'll look at the soft toys.'

But there was no soft toy they could afford – they were all much too expensive. Then Bets pounced on a set of doll's furniture, for a doll's house.

'Oh, look! Isn't it sweet! Let's get this, Daisy. Two tiny chairs, a table and a sofa – lovely! I'm sure Jane will love it.'

'How much is it?' said Daisy, looking at the price. 'We can just about manage it if I add some of my own.'

'I'll give you some of my pocket money next week,' said Bets. 'Oh, I do like these little chairs!'

Daisy bought the doll's furniture, and had it wrapped up nicely. 'Now we'll go home and write a message on a label, and take it to Jane's mother,' said Daisy. So off they went, and wrote the label. 'Many happy returns to Jane, with love from Daisy and Bets'.

Then they set off once again to call on Mrs Thomas, Zoe's sister. They came to the house, a small pretty one, set back from the road. They stopped at the gate.

Daisy was nervous. 'Now, whatever shall we do if Mrs Thomas isn't in?'

'Say we'll come again,' said Bets promptly. 'But she will be in. I can hear Jane and Dora playing in the garden.'

'What shall we say when the door is opened?' asked Daisy, still nervous.

'Just say we've got a present for little Jane, and then see what Mrs Thomas says,' said Bets, surprised to see how nervous Daisy was. '*I'll* manage this if you can't, Daisy.'

That was quite enough to make Daisy forget all her nervousness! 'I can manage it all right, thank you,' she said huffily. 'Come on!'

They went to the front door and rang the bell. Mrs Thomas opened the door. 'Hello Daisy!' she said. 'And who is this – oh, little Elizabeth Hilton, isn't it?'

'Yes,' said Bets, whose name really was Elizabeth.

'Er – it's Jane's birthday tomorrow, isn't it?' began Daisy. 'We've brought her a little present, Mrs Thomas.'

'How kind of you!' said Mrs Thomas. 'What is it?'

Daisy gave it to her. 'It's just some doll's furniture,' she said. 'Has she got a doll's house?'

'Well, isn't that strange – her daddy and I are giving Jane a doll's house tomorrow!' said Mrs Thomas. 'This furniture will be *just* right!'

'Oh – *could* we see the doll's house, please?' asked Bets at once, seeing a wonderful chance of getting into the house and talking.

'Of course,' said Mrs Thomas. 'Come in.'

So in they went and were soon being shown a lovely little doll's house in an upstairs room. Daisy led the talk round to the Little Theatre.

'You sister Zoe Summers acts in the show at the Little Theatre, doesn't she?' she said innocently.

'Yes,' said Mrs Thomas. 'Have you seen any of the shows?'

'We're going this afternoon,' said Bets. 'I do want to see that pantomime cat.'

'Poor cat!' said Mrs Thomas. 'Poor Boysie. He's in a dreadful state now – that awful policeman has been at him, you know – he thinks Boysie did that robbery. I expect you heard about it.'

Just as she said that, a tall and pretty young

129

woman came into the room. 'Hello!' she said, 'I thought I heard voices up here. Who are these friends of yours, Helen?'

'This is Daisy and this is Elizabeth, or Bets – that's what you are called, isn't it?' said Mrs Thomas, turning to Bets. 'This is Zoe – my sister – the one who acts in the show at the Little Theatre.'

Well! *What* a bit of luck! Daisy and Bets stared earnestly at Zoe. How pretty she was – and what a smiley face. They liked her very much.

'Did I hear you talking about poor Boysie?' said Zoe, sitting down by the doll's house, and beginning to rearrange the furniture in it. 'It's a shame! As if he could have done that job on Friday evening! He hasn't got the brains – he'd never, ever think of it, even to get back at the manager for his unkindness.'

'Why – is the manager unkind to Boysie?' asked Bets.

'Yes – awfully impatient with him. You see,' said Zoe, 'Boysie is slow, and he's only given silly parts like Dick Whittington's cat or Mother Goose's goose and things like that – and the manager shouts at him till poor old Boysie gets worse than ever. I couldn't bear it on Friday morning, when we had a

130

rehearsal – I flared up and told the manager what I thought of him!'

'Did you really?' said Daisy. 'Was he angry?'

'Yes, very,' said Zoe. 'We had a real shouting match, and he told me I could leave at the end of this week.'

'Oh dear,' said Daisy. 'So you've lost your job then?'

'Yes. But I don't mind. I'm tired and I want a rest,' said Zoe. 'I'm coming to stay with my sister here for a bit. We shall both like that.'

'I expect you thought it served the manager right, when he was drugged and robbed that night,' said Daisy. 'Where were you when it happened?'

'I left at half past five with the others,' said Zoe, 'and came here. I believe old Mr Goon thinks I did the robbery, with Boysie to help me!'

'But how could he, if you were here all evening?' said Bets at once. 'Didn't your sister tell Mr Goon you were here?'

'Yes – but unfortunately I went out at a quarter to seven, after I'd put the children to bed, to go to the postbox,' said Zoe. 'And my sister didn't hear me come back ten minutes later! I went up to my bedroom and stayed there till about a quarter to eight and then came down again. So, you see, according to Mr Goon, I could have slipped down to the Little Theatre, put a sleeping-draught into the manager's cup of tea, taken down the mirror, opened the safe and stolen the money – all with poor Boysie's help! *And* Mr Goon has actually found a handkerchief – it isn't mine, by the way – with a Z on it, on the verandah at the back of the theatre – and he says I dropped it when Boysie let me in that night. What do you think of *that*?'

13. LARRY AND PIP ON THE JOB

The two girls were full of horror – especially at the mention of that unfortunate handkerchief. Daisy went scarlet when she remembered how she had sewn a Z on it in one corner, never, ever thinking that there might be anyone called Zoe.

They both stared at poor Zoe, and Bets was almost in tears. Daisy wanted to blurt out about the handkerchief and how she had put the Z on it – but she stopped herself in time. She must ask Fatty's permission first.

'Mr Goon was most unpleasant,' said Mrs Thomas. 'He cross-examined me about Zoe till I was tired! He wanted to see all the navy coats in the house too – goodness knows what for!'

The two girls knew quite well! Mr Goon had got that bit of navy blue cloth that Fatty had jabbed on a nail for a false clue – and he was looking for a coat with a hole in it to match the piece of cloth! Oh dear – this was getting worse and worse.

'He also wanted to know what kind of cigarettes we smoked,' said Zoe. 'And he seemed awfully pleased when we showed him a pack off "Players"!'

Daisy's heart sank even further, and so did Bets'. It was 'Players' cigarettes whose ends Fatty had scattered over the verandah. Who would have thought that their silly, false clues would have fitted so well into this case – and, alas, fitted poor Zoe so well!

Bets blinked back her tears. She was scared and unhappy. She looked desperately at Daisy. Daisy caught the look and knew that Bets wanted to go. She wanted to go herself also. She too was scared and worried. Fatty must be told all this. He really must. He would know what to do!

So the two of them got up and said a hurried good-bye. 'We'll be seeing you this afternoon,' said Daisy to Zoe. 'We're coming to the show. Could we have your autograph, all of us, if we wait at the stage door?'

'Of course,' said Zoe. 'How many are there of you? Five? Right – I'll tell the others, if you like, and they will all give you their autographs. Mind you clap me this afternoon!'

'Oh, we will, we really will,' said Bets fervently. 'Please don't get arrested, will you?'

Zoe laughed. 'Of course not. I didn't do the robbery, and poor Boysie had nothing to do with it either. I'm quite sure of that. I'm not really afraid of that nasty Mr Goon. Don't worry!'

But the two girls did worry dreadfully as they hurried away, longing for twelve o'clock to come, so that they could tell Fatty and the others all that they had found out.

'We did very well, actually,' said Daisy, when they got to Bets' playroom and sat down to talk things over. 'Only we found out things we didn't like at all. That *handkerchief*, Bets! I do feel so guilty. I'll never, ever do a thing like that again in my life.'

Larry and Pip came along about ten to twelve. They looked pleased with themselves.

'Hello girls! How did you get on?' said Pip. 'We did very well!'

So they had. They had biked down to the Little Theatre, and had gone to the booking office to book the seats for the afternoon's show. But the office was closed.

'Let's snoop round a bit – because if anyone sees us, we can always say we've come to buy tickets, and we were looking for someone to ask,' said Pip. So they left the front of the theatre and went round to the back, trying various doors on the way. They were all locked.

They came to the car-park at the back of the theatre. A man was there, cleaning a motorbike. The boys had no idea who he was.

'That's a fine bike,' said Pip to Larry. The man heard their voices, and looked up. He was a middle-aged man, rather stout, with a thin-lipped mouth and bad-tempered lines on his forehead.

'What are you doing here?' he said.

'Well, we actually came to buy tickets for this afternoon's show,' said Larry. 'But the booking office is shut.'

'Of course it is. You can get the tickets when you come along this afternoon,' said the man, rubbing vigorously at the shining mudguards of the motorbike. 'We only open the booking office on Saturday mornings, when we expect plenty of people. Anyway, clear off now. I don't like loiterers – after that robbery on Friday I'm not putting up with anyone hanging around my theatre!'

'Oh – are you the manager, by any chance?' said Larry at once.

'Yes. I am. The man in the news! The man who was doped and robbed last Friday!' said the manager. 'If I could only get my hands on the one who did that job!'

'Have you any idea who did it?' asked Pip.

'None at all,' said the manager. 'I don't really believe it was that idiot of a Boysie. He'd never have been able to do all that. Anyway, he's too scared of me to try tricks of that sort – but he might have helped someone else do it. Someone he let in that night, when the theatre was empty!'

The boys were thrilled to hear all this first-hand information. 'It said in the paper that Boysie – the pantomime cat – brought you in your cup of tea – the one that was drugged,' said Larry. 'Did he, sir?'

'He certainly brought me in the tea,' said the manager. 'I was very busy, and only just glanced up to take it – but it was Boysie all right. He was still in his cat-skin so I couldn't mistake him. Too lazy to take it off. That's Boysie all over. I've even known him go to bed in it. But he's funny in the head, you know. Like a child. He couldn't have done the job by himself, though he must have had something to do with it – he's so easily led.'

'Then – somebody might have come back that night – been let in by Boysie – your tea might have been drugged – and taken up by Boysie to you as usual, so that you wouldn't suspect anything,' said Larry. 'And as soon as you were asleep, the one that Boysie let in must have crept up to your room, taken down the mirror, got the key from wherever you keep it, and opened the safe – and got away before you woke up.'

'That's about it,' said the manager, standing up to polish the handlebars. 'And, what's more, it must have been one of the cast, because no one knows as much about things as they do – why, whoever the thief was even knew that I didn't keep the safe key on my keyring – I always keep it in a secret pocket of my wallet. And only the cast knew that, for once, I hadn't put Thursday's takings into the bank, because they saw me coming back in a temper when I found out the bank was closed!'

The boys drank all this in. Some of it they already knew, but it sounded much more exciting and real to hear it from the lips of the manager himself. They didn't like him – he looked bad-tempered and mean. They could quite well imagine that he would have a lot of enemies who would like to pay him back for some spiteful thing he had said or done to them.

'I suppose the police are on the job all right,' said Pip, taking a duster and beginning to rub the spokes of the wheels.

'Oh yes. That constable – what's his name? – Mr Goon – has been practically *living* here this weekend – interviewing everyone. He's got poor Boysie so scared that I don't think he really knows what he's saying now. He shouts at him till Boysie bursts into tears.'

'Beast,' muttered Pip, and the manager looked at him in surprise.

'Oh, I don't know. If Boysie did it, he's got to get it out of him somehow. Anyway, it doesn't hurt him to be yelled at – only way to get things into his thick head sometimes!'

The motorbike was finished now, and shone

brightly. The manager ran it into a shed. 'Well, that's done,' he said. 'Sorry I can't give you your tickets now. You'll get them easily enough this afternoon. There are never many people on Mondays.'

The boys went off, delighted at all they had learnt. To get the whole story from the manager himself was simply marvellous. Now they knew as much as Mr Goon did! It was certainly very, very mysterious. The pantomime cat *had* taken the drugged cup of tea to the manager – and if he hadn't put the sleeping-draught into it himself, he must have known who had done it – must even have let them in. He might even have watched while the thief took down the mirror and robbed the safe. Things looked very black for Boysie. Larry and Pip could quite well imagine how Mr Goon must have shouted and yelled at him to try and make him tell the name of the robber.

'Come on – it's a quarter to twelve. Let's get back,' said Larry, who was bursting to tell his news. 'I wonder how the girls have got on. They had an easy job, really. And so had Fatty – just got to question PC Pippin, and that's all.'

'I like this detecting business, don't you?' said

Larry, as they cycled up the road. 'Of course, it's more difficult for us than for Mr Goon or PC Pippin – all they've got to do is go to anyone they like and ask questions, knowing that the people *must* answer the police – and they can go into any house they like and snoop around – but we can't.'

'No, we can't. But, on the other hand, we can perhaps pick up little bits of news that people might not tell Mr Goon,' said Pip. 'Look out – there's Mr Goon now!'

So it was – a frowning and majestic Mr Goon, riding his bicycle, and looking very important. He called out to them as he came near.

'Where's that big boy? You tell him if I see him again this morning, I'll go and complain to his parents. Poking his nose where he's not wanted! Where is he?'

'I don't know,' said Pip and Larry together, and grinned. What could Fatty have been doing now?

'You don't know! Gah! I bet you know where he's hiding, ready to pick Pippin's brains again. Does he think he's on this case too? Well, he's not. *I'm* in charge of this. You tell him that!'

And with that, Mr Goon sailed off, leaving Larry

and Pip full of curiosity to know what in the world Fatty had been doing now!

14. MORE NEWS – AND A VERY FAT FACE

Fatty had had rather a hectic morning. He had biked down to the road where Mr Goon lived, and had looked into the front room of the police cottage as he passed by. Only PC Pippin was there. Good!

Fatty leaned his bicycle against the little wall in front of the house, leaving Buster on guard. He then went down the front path, and knocked on the window of the room where PC Pippin was sitting, laboriously making out reports on this and that.

Pippin looked up and grinned. He opened the door to Fatty and took the boy into the front room.

'Any news?' said Fatty.

'Well,' said Pippin, 'there's a report on the safe and the mirror – about fingerprints. Not a single one to be found!'

'Then whoever did the job was wily,' said Fatty. 'Looks as if that rules out the pantomime cat!'

Pippin was about to speak again, when he heard

Buster barking. They both looked out of the window. Mr Goon was just dismounting from his bicycle, looking as black as thunder. Buster parked himself in the middle of the gateway, and barked deliriously, as if to say, 'Yah! Can't come in! Woof, woof! Can't come in! Yah!'

'You'd better go,' said PC Pippin, hurriedly. 'I've a bit more news for you but you must go now.'

As Buster now showed every sign of being about to attack Mr Goon, Fatty hurriedly left the house and ran up to the front gate. He picked Buster up and put him in his bicycle basket.

'What you doing here?' blustered Mr Goon. 'I've warned Pippin against you, Mr Nosey Parker. You won't get anything out of *him*! He's not on this case. He doesn't know a thing – and he wouldn't tell you if he did. Clear orf! I'm tired of that cheeky face of yours.'

'Don't be rude, Mr Goon,' said Fatty, with dignity. He hated his face being called cheeky.

'Rude! I'm not rude – just truthful,' said Mr Goon, wheeling his bicycle in at the gate. 'I tell you. I don't want to see that fat face of yours any more today! I'm a busy man, with important

144

things to do. I won't have you noseying around.'

He went in, pleased to think that Pippin had heard him treat that boy the way he ought to be treated. Aha! He, Mr Goon, was well on the way to solving a very difficult case. Got it all, he had – and for once, Frederick Algernon Trotteville was going to have his nose put out of joint. Him and his fat face!

With these pleasant thoughts to keep him company, Mr Goon went in to fire off a few sharp remarks to Pippin. Fatty, anxious to have a few more words with Pippin, rode up the road a little way, and then leaned his bicycle against a tree, putting himself the other side of the trunk so that he might watch unseen for Mr Goon to come out and ride off again. The policeman had left his bicycle against the wall of his cottage, as if he meant to come out again in a little while.

Fatty stood and brooded over Goon's rude remarks about his face. Goon thought he had a fat face, did he? All right – he'd show him one! Fatty slipped his hand into his pocket and brought out two nice new plump cheek-pads. He slipped one into each cheek, between his teeth and the fleshy part of the cheek. At once, he took on a most swollen, blown-out look.

Mr Goon came out of his house in a few minutes and mounted his bicycle. He rode slowly up the road. Fatty came out from behind his tree to show himself to Mr Goon.

'You here again?' began Goon, wobbling in rage. 'You . . .'

And then he caught sight of Fatty's enormously blown-out cheeks. He blinked and looked again. Fatty grinned, and his cheeks almost burst.

Mr Goon got off his bicycle, unable to believe his eyes, but Fatty jumped on his and sailed away. He waited in a side road, riding up and down, till he thought Mr Goon must have gone, and then cycled back to Pippin.

'It's all right,' said PC Pippin, from the window. 'He's gone to send a telegram and after that he's going to the theatre car-park to snoop round again, and then he's got to go to Loo Farm about a dog. He won't be back for some time.'

Fatty had now taken out his cheek-pads and looked quite normal again.

'I won't keep you more than a few minutes,' he told PC Pippin. 'I know you're busy. What other news have you?'

'Well, there *was* a sleeping-draught in that cup all right,' said Pippin. 'A harmless one, but strong. Traces of it were found in the cup. So that's proved all right.'

'Anything else?' enquired Fatty. 'Has the money been traced?'

'No. And it won't be either,' said Pippin. 'It was all in used notes and coins.'

'Any idea yet who did the job?' asked Fatty.

'Well, I've seen Mr Goon's notes, and if you want a *motive* for the robbery – someone with a spite against the manager – any of the company would do for the thief!' said Pippin. 'Mr Goon wasn't going to tell me anything, as you know, but he's so proud of himself for finding out so much, that he gave me his notes to read. Said it would do me good to see how an expert got to work on a case like this!'

Fatty grinned. 'Yes – the sort of thing he *would* say. But what do you mean – all the company had a spite against the manager?'

'Mr Goon interviewed the manager, and got quite a lot out of him,' said PC Pippin. 'Now – take Zoe Markham – she had a row with him that morning and got the sack. And now Lucy White

– asked him to lend her some money because her mother was ill, and he raged at her and refused. And here's Peter Watting and William Orr – they want to do a series of decent straight plays here instead of this comic stuff, and the manager laughed at them – told them they were only fit for third-rate comedy stuff. Said that third-rate people would have to be content with third-rate shows.'

'I bet they were angry,' said Fatty.

'Yes. They were furious apparently,' said Pippin. 'Almost came to blows. Threatened to harrass him if he called them third-rate again. As a matter of fact, they are quite good, especially William Orr.'

'Go on,' said Fatty. 'This is interesting. Who else has a grudge against him?'

'John James wanted a rise in his salary,' said Pippin. 'Apparently the manager had promised him this after six months' run. So he asked for it and was refused. The manager said he never promised him anything of the sort.'

'Nice amiable chap, this manager,' said Fatty with a grin. 'Always ready to help! My word, what a way to run a company! They must all hate him.'

'They do!' said Pippin. 'Even poor Boysie, the

pantomime cat, detests him. Now let me see – is that the lot? No – here's Alec Grant. He wanted permission to go and act in another show on the days he's not on here – and the manager wouldn't let him. There was an awful row about that apparently – so, you see, there are plenty of people who would very much like to pay the manager back for his spiteful treatment of them!'

'What about their alibis?' asked Fatty, after a pause to digest all this.

'All checked,' said Pippin. 'And all correct, except that there's a query about Zoe Markham, because she went out of her sister's house that evening, and nobody saw her come back; she says she went straight up to her room. So, what with that fact and the Z on the handkerchief found on the verandah, Goon's got her and Boysie down as chief suspects now!'

This wasn't very pleasant. PC Pippin bent over his papers. 'Well,' he said, 'that's all I can tell you for the present – and don't you let on I've told you either! You'd better go now – and don't forget to let me know if *you've* got anything interesting up your sleeve.'

'I haven't at the moment,' said Fatty soberly. 'Except that I hope Mr Goon was tired after his afternoon walk yesterday!'

Pippin looked up at once. 'What – trailing that redheaded foreigner! You don't mean to say he was *you*!'

'Well – I thought Mr Goon might as well meet *somebody* off the three thirty train!' said Fatty. 'You'd have thought he would have been a bit suspicious of redheads by now, wouldn't you, PC Pippin?'

And with that Fatty went off whistling on his bicycle, thinking hard. A thought struck him. He put his cheek-pads in, and rode off to the post office. Goon might still be there.

He was. Fatty sidled into the nearby phone kiosk as Mr Goon came out of the post office. The policeman saw someone grinning at him from the kiosk and stopped. He gazed in horror at Fatty, whose cheeks were now as enormous as when Goon had seen him a short time before.

Fatty nodded and grinned amiably. Goon walked off puzzled. That boy! His face seemed fatter than ever. He couldn't be blowing it out with his breath, because he was grinning. He must have some disease!

Fatty shot off on his bicycle, taking a short cut to the car-park behind the theatre. He took his bike to the shed, and bent over it. In a moment or two, Goon came sailing in on *his* bicycle, and dismounted to put it into the shed. He saw a boy there, but took no notice – till Fatty turned round and presented him with yet another wonderful view of his cheeky face.

Goon got a shock. He peered closely at Fatty. 'You got toothache?' he enquired. 'Talk about a chubby face!'

He disappeared into the theatre, and Fatty rode off to Loo Farm. He waited there for ten minutes, sitting on his bicycle behind a wall. When he spotted Goon coming along, he rode out suddenly, and once again Mr Goon got a fine view of a full moon face shining out at him.

'Now you clear orf!' yelled Mr Goon. 'Following me about like this! You with your fat face and all. You go and see a dentist. Gah! Think yourself funny, following me about with that face?'

'But Mr Goon – it looks as if you're following *me* about,' protested Fatty. 'I go to use the phone, and you are there! I go to the car-park and you come there too. And I call at Loo Farm and, hey presto, you come along here as well! What are you following ME for? Do you think *I* did the robbery at the Little Theatre?'

Mr Goon looked in puzzled distaste at Fatty's fat face. He couldn't make it out. How could anyone's face get as fat as that so suddenly? Was he seeing double?

He decided not to call at Loo Farm while that boy was hanging round with his full moon face. Mr Goon rode away down the road defeated.

'Beast!' he murmured to himself. 'Regular beast, that boy. No doing anything with him. Well, he don't know how well I've got on with this case. Give him a shock when he finds it's all cleared up, arrests been made, and sees the Inspector giving me a pat on the back! Him and his fat face!'

Fatty looked at his watch. It was getting on for twelve. He'd better go back and join the others. What news had they been able to get?

He rode up to Pip's house. They were all there, waiting for him. Bets waved out of the window.

'Hurry *up*, Fatty! We've all got plenty of news! We thought you were *never* coming!'

15. AT THE SHOW – AND AFTERWARDS

The children sat down in Pip's big playroom, a bag of chocolates between them, supplied by Larry.

'Well – it looks as if we've all got something to report,' said Fatty. 'Girls first. How did you get on, Daisy and Bets?'

Taking it in turns to supply the news, Bets and Daisy told their story. 'Wasn't it *lucky* to see Zoe herself?' said Daisy. 'She's sweet, she really is. *She* couldn't possibly have done the job, Fatty.'

'But isn't it awful about the hanky with Z on?' said Bets. 'And oh, Fatty – she smokes the same kind of cigarettes as our cigarette-ends were made of – "Players"!'

'Well, Mr Goon will probably find that most of the others smoke them too, so we needn't worry so much about that,' said Fatty. 'I'm sorry about that hanky business, though. *Why* did we put Z on that silly hanky!'

'Don't you think we ought to tell Mr Goon that – I mean, about us putting the hanky down for a false clue?' said Daisy, anxiously. 'I can't bear Mr Goon going after poor Zoe with a false clue like that – it's awful for her.'

'It can't *prove* anything,' said Fatty, thinking hard. 'If it *had* been hers, she might have dropped it any old time, not just that evening. I don't see that Mr Goon can make it really *prove* anything.'

'Neither do I,' said Larry. 'We'll own up when the case is finished – but I don't see much point in us spoiling our own chances of solving the mystery by confessing to Mr Goon.'

'All right,' said Daisy. 'Only I can't *help* feeling awful about it.'

'I must say you two girls did very well,' said Fatty. 'You got a lot of most interesting information. What about you, Larry and Pip?'

Then Larry and Pip told of their meeting with the manager, and related in great detail all he had said to them. Fatty listened eagerly. This was fantastic!

'Well – that was fine,' he said when the two boys had finished. 'I feel there's absolutely no doubt at all now that it was Boysie who took in the doped tea.

154

Well – if he *did* do the job – or helped somebody to do it – he certainly made it quite clear that he was in it, by taking the tea to the manager! I suppose he didn't realise that the remains of the tea would show the traces of the sleeping-draught. It's the sort of thing someone like Boysie would forget.'

'Well – we shall see him this afternoon,' said Daisy. 'I forgot to tell you, Fatty, that we arranged with Zoe to meet all the members of the show after it has finished this afternoon, for autographs. So we shall see Boysie as well.'

'Very good,' said Fatty pleased. 'You all seem to have done marvellously. I consider I've trained you really well!'

He was completely pummelled for that remark. When peace had been restored again, Larry asked him how *he* had got on – and he related all that Pippin had told him.

'It's funny that every single member of the show had a grudge against the manager, isn't it?' he said. 'He must be a beast. He did just the kind of things that would make people want to pay him back. Motives sticking out everywhere!'

'What are motives?' Bets wanted to know.

'Good reasons for doing something,' explained Fatty. 'Understand? The show people all had good reasons for getting back at their manager – motives for paying him back for his beastliness.'

'It's a very interesting mystery, this,' said Larry. 'Seven people could have done the job – all of them have good motives for getting even with the manager – and all of them, except Boysie, and perhaps Zoe, have good alibis. And we don't think either of those would have done the job! Zoe sounds much too nice.'

'I agree,' said Fatty. 'It's a super mystery. A proper Who-Dun-It.'

'What's *that*?' said Bets at once.

'Oh dear,' said Pip. 'Bets – a Whodunit is a mystery with a crime in it that people have got to solve – to find out who did it.'

'Well, what's it called a Whodunit for then?' said Bets, sensibly. 'I shall call it a Who-Did-It.'

'You call it what you like,' said Fatty grinning. 'So long as we find out who-dun-it or who-did-it, it doesn't matter what we call it. Now – what's the next step?'

'We'll all go to the show this afternoon, watch

everyone acting, and then go round and collect autographs, speak to all the members of the show, and take particular notice of Boysie,' said Larry, at once.

'Go up top,' said Fatty. 'And tomorrow we go after the rest of the alibis. Larry and Daisy will go to see Mary Adams, to find out if Lucy White's alibi is sound – and Pip and I will see if we can test Peter Watting's and William Orr's. We shall have to find out how to check John James too – he went to the cinema all evening – or so he said.'

'Yes – and Alec Grant's,' said Daisy. 'He went to Sheepridge and gave a show there on his own.'

'Silly to check that really,' said Pip. 'So many people heard and saw him. Anyway, it will be jolly easy to check.'

'There's Mummy calling us for dinner,' said Pip. 'I must go and wash. What time shall we meet this afternoon? And where? Down at the theatre?'

'Yes,' said Fatty. 'Be there at a quarter to three. The show starts at three. So long!'

They were all very hungry indeed for their meal. Detecting was hungry work, it seemed! Fatty spent a long time after his meal writing out all the things he knew about the mystery. It made very interesting reading indeed. Fatty read it over afterwards, and felt puzzled. So many suspects, so many motives, so many alibis – how in the world would they ever unravel them all?

At a quarter to three, all the Find-Outers were down at the Little Theatre. A young boy was in the booking office, and sold them their tickets. They passed into the theatre and found their seats. They had taken them as far forward as they could, so as to be able to observe the actors very closely.

They were in the middle of the second row – very good seats indeed. Someone was playing the piano softly. There was no band, of course, for the show was only a small one. The stage curtain shook a little in the draughts that came in each time the door was opened. The children gazed at it, admiring the marvellous sunset depicted on the great sheet.

The show began punctually. The curtain went up exactly at three o'clock, and the audience sat up in expectation.

There were two plays and a skit on Dick Whittington's Pantomime. In the first two plays, Boysie did not appear, but he came in at the last one, and the children shouted with delight as he shuffled in on all fours, dressed in the big furry skin that the boys had seen through the window on Friday night.

He was very funny. He waved to the children just as he had waved to the three boys when they had peered in to see him on Friday night. He capered about, cuddled up to Zoe Markham (who was Dick Whittington and looked very fine indeed), and was altogether quite a success.

'Zoe looks lovely,' said Larry.

'Yes – but why do the principal boys parts *always* have to be taken by girls,' said Daisy, in the interval of a change of scenery. 'Do you remember in Aladdin, it was a girl who took Aladdin's part – and in Cinderella, a girl took the part of the Prince.'

'Shh!' said Bets. 'The curtain is going up again. Oh, there's the cat! And, oh, look – his skin is splitting down by his tail!'

So it was. The cat seemed to realise this and kept feeling the hole with his front paw. 'Meeow,' he said, 'meeow!' Almost as if he was a real cat, dismayed at the splitting of his coat!

'I hope he doesn't split it all the way down,' said

Bets. 'I bet he'd get into a row with that awful manager, if he did. Oh, isn't he funny! He's pretending to go after a mouse. *Is* it a mouse?'

'Only a clockwork one,' said Daisy. 'Well, Boysie may be peculiar in his head and all that – but I think he's really clever in his acting. I do really.'

Fatty thought so too. He was wondering if anyone quite so good at acting could be as silly as people said. Well – he would see if he could talk to Boysie afterwards – then he could make up his own mind about him.

The show came to an end. The curtain came down, went up once, and came down again. It stayed down. Everyone clapped and then got up to go home. It was past five o'clock.

'Now let's rush round to the stage door,' said Fatty. 'Come on!'

So, autograph books in hand, the five of them tore round to the stage door, anxious to catch all the actors and actresses before they left.

They waited for five minutes. Then Zoe came to the door, still with some of the greasepaint on her pretty face. But she had changed into a suit now, and looked quite different.

'Come along in and meet the others inside,' she said. 'They won't be out for a few minutes and it's cold standing at that door.'

So, feeling a little nervous, the five children trooped in at the stage door and followed Zoe to a big room, where one or two of the actors were gulping down cups of tea.

Peter Watting and William Orr were there, one elderly and rather sour-looking, one young and rather miserable-looking. They didn't look nearly so fine as they had done on the stage, when Peter had been Dick's master and William had been a very dashing captain, singing a loud, jolly song of the sea, the blue, blue sea!

They nodded at the children. 'Hello, kids! Autograph hunting? Well, we're flattered, I'm sure! Hand over your books.'

The two men scribbled in each book. Then Zoe introduced them to Lucy White, a tall, gentle-looking girl who had been Dick Whittington's sweetheart in the play. She had looked really beautiful on the stage, with a great mass of flowing golden curls, which the children had admired very much. But the mass of curls now stood on a side table – a grand wig – and Lucy was seen to be a quiet, brown-haired girl with a rather worried face.

She signed the books too. Then John James came in, burly, dour, and heavy-footed, a big man, just right for the king in the play. 'Hello!' he said. 'You don't mean to say that somebody wants our autographs! Well, well! Here's fame for you!'

He signed the books too. Fatty began to get into conversation with William and Peter. Larry tried to talk to John James. Pip looked round. Surely there should be somebody else to ask to sign their books?

There was – and he came in at that moment, a small, dapper little man, who had played the part of Dick's mother on the stage. He had been very good as the mother – neat and nimble, using an amusing high voice, and even singing two or three songs in a woman's voice very cleverly indeed.

'Could we have your autograph please?' said Fatty, going up to him. 'I did like your performance. I could have sworn you were a woman! Even your voice!'

'Yes – Alec was in great form with his singing today,' said Zoe. 'Got his high notes beautifully! You should see him imitate me and Lucy – imitates us really well, so that you'd hardly know it wasn't us! We tell him he's lost in this little company. He ought to be in the West End!'

'He thinks that himself, don't you Alec?' said John James, in a slightly mocking voice. 'But the manager doesn't agree with him.'

'Don't talk to me about *him*,' said Alec. 'We all detest the fellow. Here you are, kids – catch! And I hope you can read my signature!'

He threw them their books. Fatty opened his and saw a most illegible scrawl that he could just make out to be 'Alec Grant' – but only just.

Zoe laughed. 'He always writes like that. Nobody can ever read his writing. I tell him he might just as well write "Hot Potatoes" or "Peppermint Creams" and nobody would know the difference. I wonder your mother can ever read your letters, Alec.'

'She can't,' said Alec. 'She waits till I get home and then she gets me to read them to her. And I can't!'

Everyone laughed. 'Well, so long,' said Alec, winding a yellow scarf round his neck. 'See you tomorrow. And mind none of you knock the manager on the head tonight!'

16. THE PANTOMIME CAT
HAS A TEA PARTY

The children thought they ought to go too. Fatty felt as if they had stayed too long already. Then he remembered something.

'Oh – what about the pantomime cat? We haven't got *his* autograph. Where is he?'

'Clearing up the stage, I expect,' said Zoe. 'That's one of his jobs. But he won't sign your albums for you – poor old Boysie can't write.'

'Can't he, *really*?' said Bets, in amazement. 'But I thought he was grown-up – isn't he?'

'Yes – he's twenty-four,' said Zoe. 'But he's like a kid of six. He can hardly read either. But he's a dear, he really is. I'll go and get him for you.'

But before she could go, the pantomime cat came in. He walked on his hind legs, and had thrown back the furry cat-skin head, so that it looked like a grotesque hood.

He had a big head, small eyes, set too close

together, teeth that stuck out in front like a rabbit's, and a very scared expression on his face.

He came up to Zoe and put his hand in hers like a child. 'Zoe,' he said. 'Zoe must help Boysie.'

'What is it, Boysie?' said Zoe, speaking as if Boysie was a child. 'Tell Zoe.'

'Look,' said Boysie, and turned himself round dolefully. Everyone looked – and saw a big split in poor Boysie's cat-skin, near the tail. It had got much bigger since Bets had noticed it.

'And look,' said Boysie, pointing to a split down his tummy. 'Zoe can mend it for Boysie?'

'Yes Boysie, of course,' said Zoe kindly, and the cat slipped his hand in hers again, smiling up at her. He only reached to her shoulder. 'You're getting fat, Boysie,' said Zoe. 'Eating too much, and splitting your skin!'

Boysie now saw the children for the first time and smiled at them with real pleasure. 'Children,' he said, pointing at them. 'Why are they here?'

'They came to talk to us, Boysie,' said Zoe. ('He wouldn't understand what I meant if I said you wanted autographs,' she whispered to Fatty.)

Peter Watting and William Orr, tall and thin,

now said good-bye and went. Lucy White followed, leaving her wig of golden curls behind. Boysie put it on and ran round the room grinning, looking perfectly dreadful.

'See? He's just like a six-year-old, isn't he?' said Zoe. 'But he's so simple and kind – does anything he can for any of us. He's very clever with his fingers – he can carve wood beautifully. Look – here are some of the things Boysie has made for me.'

She took down a row of small wooden animals, most beautifully carved. Boysie, still in his golden wig, came and stood by them, smiling with pleasure.

'Boysie! I think they're *beautiful*,' said Bets, overcome with admiration. 'How *do* you do such lovely carving? Oh, *look* at this little lamb – it's perfect.'

Boysie suddenly ran out of the room. He came back with another little lamb, rather like the one Bets admired. He pressed it into her hand, smiling foolishly, his small eyes full of tears.

'You have this,' he said. 'I like you.'

Bets turned and looked at him. She did not see the ugly face, the too-close eyes, the big-toothed mouth. She only saw the half-scared kindness that lay behind them all. She gave him a sudden hug, thinking of him as if he were a child much younger and smaller than herself.

'There! See how pleased the little girl is,' said Zoe. 'That's nice of you, Boysie.'

She turned to the others. 'He's always like that,' she said. 'He'd give away the shirt off his back if he could. You can't help liking him, can you?'

'No,' said everyone, and it was true. Boysie was funny in the head and silly, he was ugly to look at – but he was kind and sincere and humble, he had a sense of fun – and you simply *couldn't* help liking him.

'I can't bear it when people are unkind to Boysie,' said Zoe. 'Sometimes the manager is, and I just see red then. I did last Friday, didn't I Boysie?'

Boysie's face clouded over and he nodded. 'You mustn't go away,' he said to Zoe, and put his hand in hers. 'You mustn't leave Boysie.'

'He says that because the manager gave me notice on Friday,' said Zoe. 'He's afraid I'll go. But I won't. The manager doesn't want to lose me really – though I'd like a bit of a rest. But he said this afternoon he didn't mean what he said last Friday.

He's a funny one. Nobody likes him.'

'I say – I suppose we really ought to go,' said Fatty. 'Are you coming, Zoe – may we call you Zoe?'

'Of course,' said Zoe. 'Well, no, I won't go yet. I must mend Boysie's cat-skin. I'll stay and have tea with him, I think. I say, Boysie – shall we ask all these nice children to stay to tea too?'

Boysie was thrilled. He stroked Zoe's arm, and then took Bets' hand. 'Boysie will make tea,' he said. 'You sit down.'

'Boysie, aren't you going to take off your cat-skin?' asked Zoe. 'You'll be so hot – and you might split it even more.'

Boysie paid no attention. He went off into a small cupboard-like place, and they heard him filling a kettle.

'We'd *love* to stay,' said Fatty, who thought Zoe was just about the nicest person he had ever seen. 'If we're no bother. Shall I pop out and buy some buns?'

'Yes. That would be a lovely idea,' said Zoe. 'Where's my purse? I'll give you the money.'

'I've plenty, thank you,' said Fatty hastily. 'I won't be long! Coming Larry?'

He and Larry disappeared. Boysie watched for the kettle to boil, which it soon did. Just as he turned it off, Fatty and Larry came back with a collection of jammy buns, chocolate cakes and ginger biscuits.

'There's a plate in the cupboard where Boysie is,' said Zoe. 'My word – what a feast!'

Fatty went into the little cupboard. He watched Boysie with interest. The little fellow, still in his cat-skin, had warmed the brown teapot. He now tipped out the water from the pot and put in some tea.

'How many spoons of tea, Zoe?' he called.

'Oh, four will do,' said Zoe. 'Count them for him, will you? – he can't count very well.'

'I can count four,' said Boysie indignantly, but proceeded to put five in instead. Then he poured boiling water into the pot and put the lid on.

'Do you make tea every evening?' asked Fatty, and Boysie nodded.

'Yes. He's good at making tea,' said Zoe, as Boysie carried the teapot in and set it down on the table. 'He usually makes it for us as soon as the show is over – and then he makes some for the manager much later. Don't you Boysie?'

To the children's alarm, Boysie suddenly burst into tears. 'I didn't take him his tea. I didn't,' he wept.

'He's remembering about last Friday,' said Zoe, patting Boysie comfortingly. 'That policeman keeps on and on at him, trying to make him say he took a cup of tea to the manager and Boysie keeps saying he didn't. Though the manager says he *did*. I expect Boysie has got muddled and has forgotten.'

'Tell us about it, Boysie,' said Fatty, rather thrilled at getting so much first-hand information. 'You don't need to worry about talking to *us*. We're your friends. We know you didn't have anything to do with what happened on Friday night.'

'I didn't, did I?' said Boysie, looking at Zoe. 'You all went, Zoe. You didn't stay with Boysie like today. I was in my cat-skin because it's hard to take off by myself. You know it is. And I went into the back room where there's a fire!'

'He means the room behind the verandah,' explained Zoe. 'There's an electric fire there that Boysie likes to sit by.'

'And I saw you – and you – and you,' said Boysie surprisingly, poking his paw at Fatty, Larry, and Pip. 'Not you,' he added, poking Bets and Daisy.

'You never said that before,' said Zoe in surprise. 'That's naughty, Boysie. You *didn't* see these children.'

'I did. They looked in the window,' said Boysie. 'I looked at them too. I frightened them! They looked again and I waved to them to tell them not to be frightened, because they are nice children.'

The five children looked at one another. *They* knew that Boysie was telling the truth. He *had* seen them that Friday night – he *had* waved to them.

'Did you tell the policeman this?' asked Fatty suddenly.

Boysie shook his head. 'No. Boysie didn't remember then. Remembers now.'

'What did you do after the children had gone?' asked Fatty gently.

'I made some tea,' said Boysie, screwing up his face to remember. 'Some for me and some for the manager.'

'Did you drink yours first?' asked Fatty. 'Or did you take *his* up first?'

'Mine was hot,' said Boysie. 'Very hot. Too hot. I played till it was cool, then I drank it.'

'*Then* did you pour out the manager's tea and

take it to him?' asked Fatty. Boysie blinked his eyes and a hunted look came over his face.

'No,' he said. 'No, no, no! I didn't take it, I didn't, I didn't! I was tired. I lay down on the rug and I went to sleep. But I didn't take the tea upstairs. Don't make me say I did. I didn't, I didn't.'

There was a long pause. Everyone was wondering what to say. Fatty spoke first.

'Have a jammy bun everyone. Here, Boysie, there's an extra-jammy one for you – and don't you bother any more about that tea. Forget it!'

17. CHECKING UP THE ALIBIS

No more was said about Friday evening after that. It was quite clear that talking about it upset Boysie terribly. Fatty was very puzzled indeed. Boysie *had* taken up the tea – the manager said so quite definitely because, as now, he was still in his cat-skin and was quite unmistakable. Then what was the point of Boysie denying it? Was he trying to shield somebody in his foolish way, by denying everything to do with the doped cup of tea?

If so – who was he trying to shield? Zoe? No! Nobody could possibly suspect Zoe of drugging anyone's tea, or robbing a safe. Nobody – except Mr Goon!

It was imperative to check up on all the other alibis. If there was a single chink in any of them, that was probably the person Boysie was trying to shield. Fatty made up his mind that every other alibi must be gone into the next day without fail. If he couldn't find something definite, it looked as if the poor old pantomime cat would be arrested, and Zoe too! Because Mr Goon would be sure that Zoe, whom Boysie obviously adored, was the person he was shielding.

It was a curious tea party, but the children enjoyed it. Towards the end, a loud voice came down the stairs outside the room.

'What's all the row down there? Who's there? I can hear *your* voice, Zoe!'

Zoe went to the door. 'Yes, I'm here. I'm stopping behind to mend Boysie's cat-skin. It's all split. And there are a few children here too, who came for our autographs. They're having a cup of tea with me and Boysie.'

'You tell them to be careful Boysie doesn't put something in their tea then!' shouted the manager, and went back to his room, banging the door loudly.

'Pleasant fellow, isn't he?' said Larry. 'We met him this morning. A very nasty bit of work.'

'I couldn't agree more,' said Zoe. 'Well dears, you'd better go. Get out of your skin, Boysie, if you want me to mend it.'

The children said good-bye, shaking hands with both Zoe and Boysie. Boysie looked intensely pleased at all this ceremony. He bowed each time he shook hands.

'A pleasure,' he said to each of them. 'A pleasure!'

They all went to get their bikes, which they had left in the stand inside the shed. 'Well! Fancy getting asked inside, meeting everyone, and having tea with Zoe and Boysie!' said Fatty, pleased.

'Yes. And hearing his own story,' said Larry, pushing his bike out into the yard. 'Do you believe him, Fatty?'

'Well, I know it's quite impossible that he shouldn't have taken in that cup of tea, but yet I feel Boysie's speaking the truth,' said Fatty. 'I've never been so puzzled in my life. One minute I think one thing and the next I think another.'

'Well, *Zoe* didn't do it,' said Bets loyally. 'She's much, much, much too nice.'

'I agree with you,' said Fatty. 'She couldn't have done that robbery any more than *you* could, Bets. Well, we must look elsewhere, that's all. We must check all the rest of the alibis tomorrow without fail.'

So, the next morning, the Find-Outers started off with their checking. Larry and Daisy set off to Mary Adams' flat, to find out about the gentle Lucy White. Fatty and Pip went off by the river, to find 'The Turret' and discover if William Orr and Peter Watting *had* been there on Friday night, as they said.

'Then we'll check up on John James and the cinema if we can this afternoon,' said Fatty, 'And on Alec Grant as well, if we've time. We'll have to look lively now, because it seems to me that Mr Goon will move soon. If he sees that poor Boysie any more he'll send him *right* off his head!'

Daisy found a half-embroidered cushion cover which she had never finished. She took the silks that went with it and wrapped the whole lot up in a parcel. 'Come along,' she said to Larry. 'We'll soon find out about Lucy White – though, honestly, I think it's a waste of time checking *her* alibi. She doesn't look as if she could say boo to a goose!'

They arrived at Mary Adams' flat and went upstairs to her front door. They rang, and the old lady opened the door.

'Well, well, well – *what* a surprise,' she said,

pleased. 'Daisy *and* Larry. It's a long time since I've seen you – what enormous children you've grown into. You come along in.'

She led the way into her tiny sitting-room. She took down a tin of chocolate biscuits from the mantelpiece and offered them one. She was a small, white-haired old lady, almost crippled with rheumatism now, but still able to sew and knit.

Daisy opened her parcel. 'Mary, do you think you could possibly finish this cushion cover for me before Easter? I want to give it to Mummy, and I know I shan't have time to finish it myself, because I'm embroidering her some hankies too. How much would you charge for doing it for me?'

'Not a penny, Daisy,' said Mary Adams, beaming. 'It would be a pleasure to do something for you, and especially something that's going to be given to your dear mother. Bless your dear heart, I'd love to finish it just for love and nothing else.'

'Thank you so much Mary,' said Daisy. 'It's very kind of you – and I'll bring you some of our daffodils as soon as they're properly out. They're very behind this year.'

'Have another biscuit?' said Mary, taking down

the tin again. 'Well, it *is* nice to see you both. I've been ill, you know, and haven't been out much. So it's a real change to see a visitor or two.'

'Do you know Lucy White?' said Larry. 'We got her autograph this afternoon. She's a friend of yours, isn't she?'

'Yes – dear Lucy! She came to see me every night last week, when I was bad,' said Mary. 'I had a lot of knitting to finish and that kind girl came in and helped me till it was all done.'

'Did she come on Friday too?' asked Daisy.

'Ah – you're like that Mr Goon – he's been round here three times asking questions about Friday evening,' said Mary. 'Yes, Lucy came along about quarter to six, and we sat and knitted till half past nine, when she went home. We heard the nine o'clock news, and she made us some cocoa, with some biscuits, and we had *such* a nice time together.'

Well, that seemed pretty definite.

'Didn't Lucy leave you at all, till half past nine?' said Daisy.

'Not once. She didn't so much as go out of the room,' said Mary. 'There we sat in our chairs, knitting away for dear life – and the next day, Lucy took all the knitting we'd done that week and delivered it for me. She's a good kind girl.'

There came a ring at the door. 'I'll go for you,' said Daisy and got up. She opened the door – and there was Mr Goon, red in the face from climbing the steps to Mary's flat! He glared suspiciously at Daisy.

'What are *you* doing here?' he demanded. 'Poking your noses in?'

'We came to ask Mary to do some sewing,' said Daisy, in a dignified voice.

'Oh yes!' said Mr Goon, disbelievingly. 'Mary Adams in?'

'Yes I am,' called Mary Adams' voice, sounding rather cross. 'Is that you again, Mr Goon? I've nothing more to say to you. Please go away. Wasting my time like this!'

'I just want to ask you a few more questions,' said Mr Goon, walking into the little sitting-room.

'Theophilus Goon, since you were a nasty little boy *so* high, you've always been a one for asking snoopy questions,' said Mary Adams, and the two children heard Mr Goon snort angrily. They called good-bye and fled away, laughing.

'I bet he *was* a nasty little boy too!' said Larry, as they went down the stairs. 'Well, that was easy, Daisy.'

'Very,' said Daisy. 'And quite definite too. It rules out Lucy White. I do wonder how the others are getting on.'

Bets was waiting at home with Buster. She had wanted to go with Pip and Fatty, but Fatty had said no, she had better stay with Buster. He and Pip had gone off down by the river, taking the road along which William Orr and Peter Watting had said they went.

They came to a tall and narrow house, with a little turret. On the gate was its name. 'The Turret. Coffee, sandwiches, snacks.'

'Well, here we are,' said Fatty. 'We'll try the coffee, sandwiches, snacks. I feel very hungry.'

So in they went and found a nice table looking out on a primrose garden. A small girl came to serve them. She didn't look more than about twelve, though she must have been a good deal older.

'Coffee for two, please,' said Fatty. 'And sandwiches. And something snacky.'

The girl laughed. 'I'll bring you a tray of snacks,' she said. 'Then you can help yourselves.'

She brought them two cups of hot, steaming coffee, a plate of egg, potted meat, and cress sandwiches, and a tray of delicious-looking snacks.

'Ha! *We've* chosen the right place to come and check up on alibis,' said Fatty, eyeing the tray with delight. 'Look at all this!'

The boys ate the sandwiches, and then chose a snack. It was delicious. 'Come on – let's carry on with the snacks,' said Fatty. 'We've had a long walk and I'm hungry. I don't care if I *do* spoil my dinner – it's a really good way to spoil it – most enjoyable.'

'But have you got enough money to pay, Fatty?' asked Larry anxiously. 'I haven't got much on me.'

'Plenty,' said the wealthy Fatty, and rattled his pockets. 'We'll start on checking the alibi as soon as we've finished our meal. Hello – LOOK who's here!'

It was Mr Goon! He walked in as if he owned the place, and then he saw Fatty!

18. MORE CHECKING –
AND A FEW SNACKS

Mr Goon advanced on Fatty's table. 'Everywhere I go,' boomed Mr Goon, 'I see some of you kids. Now, what are you doing *here*?'

'Eating,' said Fatty politely. 'Did you come in for a snack too, Mr Goon? Not much left, unfortunately.'

'You hold your tongue,' said Mr Goon.

'But you asked me a question,' objected Fatty. 'You said . . .'

'I know what I said,' said Mr Goon. 'I'm fed up with you kids! I go to Mary Adams and I see some of you there. I come here and here you are again. And I bet when I go somewhere else, you'll be there as well! Lot of pests you are.'

'It's funny how often we see *you* too, Mr Goon,' said Fatty, in the pleasant, polite voice that always infuriated Mr Goon. 'Quite a treat.'

Mr Goon swelled up and his face went purple.

Then the little girl came into the room, and he turned to her pompously. 'Is your mother in? I want a word with her.'

'No, she's not, sir,' said the little girl. 'I'm the only one here. Mother will be back soon, if you would like to wait.'

'I can't wait,' said Mr Goon, annoyed. 'Too much to do. I'll come tomorrow.'

He was just going when he turned to look at Fatty. He had suddenly remembered his fat cheeks. They didn't seem nearly so fat now.

'What you done to make your cheeks thin?' he said suspiciously.

'Well – I *might* have had all my back teeth out,' said Fatty. 'Let me see – did I Larry? Do you remember?'

'Gah!' said Mr Goon, and went. The little girl laughed uproariously.

'Oh, you are funny!' she said. 'You really are. Isn't he horrid? He came and asked Mummy and me ever so many questions about two men that came here last Friday night.'

'Oh yes,' said Fatty, at once. 'I know the men – actors, aren't they? I've got their autographs in

183

my autograph album. Were they here on Friday then? I bet they liked your snacks.'

'Yes, they came on Friday,' said the little girl. 'I know, because it was my birthday, and Peter Watting brought me a book. I'd just been listening to Radio Fun at half past six, when they came in.'

'Half past six,' said Fatty. 'Well, what did they do then? Eat all your snacks?'

'No! They only had coffee and sandwiches,' said the little girl. 'They gave me the book – it's a beauty, I'll show you – and then we listened to Radio Theatre at seven o'clock. And then something went wrong with the radio and it stopped.'

'Oh,' said Fatty disappointed, because he had been counting on the radio for checking up on the time. 'What happened then?'

'Well, Peter Watting's very good with radios,' said the little girl. 'So he said he'd try and mend it. Mummy said, "Mend it in time for eight o'clock then, because I want to hear a concert then".'

'And was it mended by then?' asked Fatty.

'No. Not till twenty past eight,' said the little girl. 'Mummy was very disappointed. But we got it going by then, quite all right – twenty past eight, I mean – and then Peter and William had to go. They caught the ferry and went across the river.'

This was all very interesting. It certainly proved beyond a doubt that William Orr and Peter Watting could not possibly have had anything to do with the robbery at the Little Theatre. That was certain. The little girl was quite obviously telling the truth.

'Well, thanks for a really good tea,' said Fatty. 'How much do we owe you?'

The little girl gave a squeal. 'Oh, I never counted your snacks. Do you know how many you had? I shan't half be in trouble with Mummy if she knows I didn't count.'

'Well, you ought to count,' said Fatty. 'It's too much like hard work for us to count when we're eating. Larry, I make it six snacks each, the sandwiches and the coffee. Is that correct?'

It was. Fatty paid up, gave the little girl a coin to buy herself something for the birthday she had had on Friday, and went off with Larry, feeling decidedly full.

'We've just got time to go to the cinema to see if we can pick up anything about John James' visit,' said Fatty. 'Oh dear – I wish I hadn't snacked quite so much. I don't feel very brainy at the moment.'

They went into the little lobby. There was a girl at a table, marking off piles of tickets.

'Good morning,' said Fatty. 'Er – could you tell us anything about last week's programme?'

'Why? Are you thinking of going to it?' said the girl, with a giggle. 'You're a bit late.'

'My friend and I have been having a bit of an argument about it,' said Fatty, making this up on the spur of the moment, while Larry looked at him in surprise. 'You see, my friend thinks the programme was *The Yearling* and I said it was – er – er – *Henry V*.'

'No, no,' said the girl graciously. 'It was *The Weakling*, not *The Yearling*, and *Henry the Fifteenth*, not *Henry V*.'

Fatty turned crossly and went out. He bumped into somebody coming up the steps.

He nearly fell, and clutched hold of the person he had collided with. A familiar voice grated in his ear.

'Take your hands off me! Wherever I go, I find one of you kids! What you doing *here*, I'd like to know?'

186

'They wanted to buy tickets for last week's programme,' called the girl from inside, and screamed with laughter. 'Cheek! I told them off all right.'

'That's right,' said Mr Goon. 'They want telling off. Coming and bothering you with silly questions.' Then it suddenly struck him that Fatty was coming about the same thing as he was – to check up on an alibi. He swung in a rage. 'Poking your n . . .' he began.

But Fatty had gone, and so had Larry. They were not going to stay and argue with Mr Goon and that girl.

'Cheek,' said Fatty, who was not easily outdone in any conversation. 'I'm afraid Mr Goon will get a lot more out of her than we shall.'

'Yes. We've rather fallen down on this alibi,' said Larry – and then he stopped and gave Fatty a sudden punch. 'I say – I know! We can ask Kitty, Pip's cook. She goes to the pictures every single Friday. She told Bets so one day and I heard her. She said she hadn't missed going for nine years.'

'Well, I bet she missed last Friday for the first

time then,' said Fatty, gloomily. The cinema girl's cheek was still rankling. 'Anyway, we'll ask and see.'

'Well, thank goodness we're not likely to run into Mr Goon in Pip's kitchen,' said Larry.

They arrived at Pip's, and went into the kitchen. Kitty beamed at them, especially at Fatty, whom she thought was very clever indeed.

'Kitty, could we possibly have a drink of water?' began Fatty.

'You shall have some homemade lemonade,' said Kitty. 'And would you like a snack to go with it?'

The very idea of a snack made Fatty turn pale. 'No thanks,' he said. 'I've just had a snack, Kitty.'

'Well, do have another,' said Kitty, and brought out some small but very tempting-looking sausage-rolls. Fatty groaned and turned away.

'Sorry, Kitty – they look marvellous – but I'm too full of snacks to risk another.'

There was a pause while Kitty filled lemonade glasses.

'Did you go to the pictures last week?' said Larry. 'You always do, don't you?'

'Never missed for nine years,' said Kitty proudly.

'Yes, I went on Friday, same as usual. Oooh, it was a *lovely* film.'

'What was it?' asked Fatty.

'Well, I went in at six and the news was on,' said Kitty. 'Then a cartoon, you know. Made me laugh like anything. Then at half past six till the end of the programme there was *He Loved Her So*. Oooh, it was *lovely*. Made me cry ever so.'

'A really happy evening,' said Fatty. 'See anyone you know?'

Kitty considered. 'No, I don't know as I did. I always get kind of wrapped up in the film, you know. It was a pity it broke down.'

Fatty pricked up his ears. 'What do you mean – broke down?'

'Well, you know what I mean, Frederick,' said Kitty. 'The picture sort of snaps – and stops – and there's only the screen, and no picture. I suppose the film breaks or something.'

'Did it do that a lot?' asked Fatty.

'Yes – four times,' said Kitty. 'All the way through, it seemed. Just at the wrong bits too – you know, the really exciting bits! Everyone was grumbling about it.'

'Pity,' said Fatty, getting up. 'Well, Kitty, thanks very much for the lemonade – and I hope you enjoy your film *this* Friday.'

'Oooh I shall,' said Kitty. 'It's called *Three Broken Hearts.*'

'You'll weep like anything,' said Fatty. 'You *will* enjoy that, Kitty. It's a pity I'll be too busy to come and lend you my hanky.'

'Oh, you are a rascal,' said Kitty, delighted.

'Come on, Larry,' said Fatty, and he pulled him out of Kitty's kitchen. 'We've learnt something there! Now, if we can only get hold of John James and find out it *he* noticed the breaks in the film – which he must have done if he was there – we shall be able to check *his* alibi all right!'

'So we shall,' said Larry. 'Jolly good work. But how can we get hold of John James? We can't just walk up to him and say, "Did you notice the breaks in the film, Mr James, when you were at the cinema on Friday?" '

'Of course we can't,' said Fatty. 'Gosh, it's almost time for dinner. We'll have to do that afterwards, Larry. Can you possibly eat any dinner? I can't.'

'No, I can't – and it's hot roast pork and apple

sauce today,' said Larry with a groan. 'What a waste.'

'Don't even *mention* roast pork,' said Fatty with a shudder. 'Why did we eat so many snacks? Now my mother's going to worry because I can't eat a thing at dinner today – take my temperature or something!'

'What about John James?' said Larry. 'How are we going to tackle him? We don't even know where to find him. He won't be at the theatre because there's no show this afternoon.'

'I'll ring Zoe when I get home and see if she knows where we can get hold of him,' said Fatty. 'We'd better take Bets too. She'll be feeling left out if we don't.'

'Right,' said Larry. 'See you this afternoon sometime.'

19. JOHN JAMES AND THE CINEMA

Very fortunately for Fatty his mother was not in for lunch, so he was able to eat as little as he liked without anyone noticing. He was only at the table about five minutes and then he went to ring Zoe, hoping she was at her sister's as usual.

She was. 'Oh – hello, Zoe,' said Fatty. 'Can you tell me something? I want to have a talk with John James, if I can. Do you know if he'll be anywhere about this afternoon?'

'Well – let me see,' said Zoe's clear voice over the telephone. 'I did hear him say something about going across the river in the ferry, and taking a picnic tea up on the hill beyond. There's a marvellous view up there, you know.'

'Yes. I know,' said Fatty. 'Oh good – I'll slip across and see if I can spot him there. Do you know what time he is going?'

Zoe didn't know. Then she told Fatty that Mr

Goon was going to see poor Boysie again that evening. 'And I heard him say that he's not going to stand any nonsense this time – Boysie's got to "come clean," the horrid fellow,' said Zoe, indignantly. 'As if he can make Boysie confess to something he doesn't know anything about!'

Fatty frowned as he hung up the receiver. He was afraid that Boysie *might* confess to the robbery, out of sheer terror and desperation. What a dreadful thing that would be – to have him confess to something he hadn't done – and have the real culprit go scot-free.

Fatty rang Larry, and then Pip, telling them of John James's plans for the afternoon. 'We've got to go and check up on his alibi,' he said. 'And we can only do that by questioning *him* – to see if he really was at the cinema on Friday night. And as it's a lovely day, let's all take our tea and go for a picnic up on the hill across the river, and kill two birds with one stone – enjoy ourselves, and do a spot of detecting as well!'

The others thought this was a splendid idea. 'Fatty always thinks of such nice things,' said Bets, happily. 'It will be lovely up there on the hills.'

Fatty had told Pip to go and ask Kitty once more about the breaks in the film on Friday night, just to make sure he had got it quite right. 'Ask if she remembers *exactly* how many breaks there were, when they came – and, if possible, the *time*,' said Fatty. 'Write it down, Pip, in case you forget the details. This may be important. It looks as if John James is our only hope now – I feel that we must count Alec Grant out, with his alibi of over a hundred people.'

The children met at the ferry at a quarter to three, laden with picnic-bags. Pip carried a mackintosh-rug. 'Mummy made me,' he said crossly. 'She said the grass is still damp. You're lucky to have a mother that doesn't fuss about things like that.'

'Mine fusses about other things,' said Fatty. 'And Larry's fusses about certain things too. Never mind, it's not much bother to sit down on a rug!'

'As a matter-of-fact,' said Bets, seriously, 'I've met one or two mothers who never fussed about their children – but, you know, I'm sure it was because they didn't care about them. I think I'd rather have a fussy mother really.'

'Here's the boat,' said Fatty, as the ferryman came rowing across. 'I'll pay for everyone. It's not much.'

They got into the boat. 'Rowed anyone across yet this afternoon?' asked Fatty. The boatman shook his head. 'No, not yet. Bit early.'

'Then John James hasn't gone across yet,' said Fatty to the others. 'Hey, Buster – don't take a header into the water, will you?'

They got across and made their way over a field and up a steep hill to the top. Fatty chose a place from where they could see the ferry.

'We'll watch and see when the ferryman goes out,' he said. 'I don't know if we could make out John James from here, but I expect we could. He's so burly.'

The spring sun was hot. The cowslips around nodded their yellow heads in the breeze. It was very pleasant up there on the hill. Larry yawned and lay down.

'You watch for J.J., you others,' he said. 'I'm going to have a nap!'

But he hadn't been asleep for more than ten minutes when Fatty prodded him in the middle.

'Wake up, Larry. Can you see if that's John James standing on the opposite side of the river, waiting for the ferry?'

Larry sat up. He had very keen eyes. He screwed them up and looked hard. 'Yes, I think it is,' he said. 'Let's hope he comes this way. I don't feel like walking miles after him.'

Fortunately it *was* John James, and he *did* come that way. The children watched him get into the boat, land on their side of the river, and follow the same path as they had taken themselves.

'Now,' said Fatty, getting up, 'we'd better start wandering about till we see where he's going to sit. Then we'll settle somewhere near.'

'How are we going to start the checking up?' asked Pip.

'I'll start it,' said Fatty. 'And then you can all follow my lead, and ask innocent questions. Roll up your rug, Pip.'

The five children and Buster wandered about and picked cowslips, keeping a sharp eye on John James, who was coming very slowly up the hill. He found a sheltered place with a bush behind him, and lay down at full length, his arms behind his head so that he could look down the hill towards the river.

Fatty wandered near him. 'Here's a good place,' he called to the others. 'We'll have the rug here.' Then he turned politely to the man nearby.

'I hope we shan't disturb you if we sit just here,' he said.

'Not if you don't yell and screech,' said John James. 'But I don't suppose you will. You look as if you've all been well brought up.'

'I hope we have,' said Fatty, and beckoned to the others. Pip put down the rug. By this time the man was sitting up, and had put a cigarette in his mouth. He patted himself all over and frowned.

'I suppose,' he said to Fatty, 'I suppose you haven't got matches on you, by any chance? I've left mine at home.'

Fatty always had every conceivable thing on him, on the principle that you simply never knew what you might want at any time. He presented John James with a full box of matches at once.

'Keep the whole box,' said Fatty. 'I'm not going to be a smoker at all.'

'Good boy,' said John James. 'Very sensible.

Thanks, old chap. I say – haven't I seen you before?'

'Yes,' said Fatty. 'We came into the back of the theatre yesterday – and you were good enough to sign our autograph albums.'

'Oh yes – now I remember you all,' said John James. 'Have you come up here for a picnic?'

'Yes. We're just about to begin,' said Fatty, though it was really much too early. But the effect of the snacks was beginning to wear off, and the lack of a midday meal was making itself felt! Fatty was more than ready for a picnic. 'Er – I suppose you wouldn't like to join us – we've got plenty.'

'Yes. I will,' said John James. 'I've got some stuff here too. We'll pool it.'

It was a very nice picnic, with plenty to eat, and some of Kitty's homemade lemonade to drink. For a short while, Fatty and the others talked about whatever came into their heads.

Then Fatty began his 'checking'. 'What's on at the cinema this week, Larry?' he asked.

Larry told him. 'Oh no,' said Fatty, 'that was last week!'

'You're wrong,' said John James at once. 'It was *Here Goes*, the first part of the week, and *He Loved*

Her So, the second. Both absolutely dreadful.'

'Really?' said Fatty. 'I heard that *He Loved Her So* was good. But I didn't see it. I suppose you did?'

'Yes. Saw it on Friday,' said John James. 'At least – I *would* have seen it, but it was so boring that I fell asleep nearly all the time!'

This remark disappointed all the Find-Outers very much indeed. If John James slept all the time, he wouldn't have noticed the breaks in the film – and so they wouldn't be able to check his alibi.

'Hope you didn't snore!' said Fatty. 'But I suppose people would wake you up if you did.'

'I did keep waking up,' said John James. 'I kept on waking because of people talking and sounding annoyed. I don't quite know what happened – I think the film must have broken unexpectedly – like they do sometimes, you know – and that made the audience fidgety and cross. But I soon went to sleep again.'

'Bad luck, to be woken up like that!' laughed Fatty. 'I hope you didn't get disturbed from your nap *too* many times!'

John James considered. 'Well, I should think that wretched film must have gone wrong at least four times,' he said. 'I remember looking at the clock once or twice – once I got woken up at quarter to seven, and another time at ten past. I remember wondering where on earth I was when I woke up then. Thought I was in bed at home!'

'Bit of a boring evening for you,' said Fatty, watching Pip take out his notebook and do a bit of checking up on times. He nodded reassuringly to Fatty. Yes, John James's alibi was safe all right. There was no doubt at all that he had been in the cinema that evening, and had been awakened each time the film broke, by the noise of the impatient people around him.

'Yes. It was boring,' said John James. 'But it was something to do. Help yourself to my cherry cake. There's plenty.'

The talk turned to the robbery at the theatre.

'Who do *you* think did it?' asked Fatty.

'I haven't a notion,' said John James. 'Not a notion. Boysie didn't. I'm sure of that. He hasn't the brains or the pluck for a thing of that sort. He's a harmless sort of fellow. He just adores Zoe – and I'm not surprised. She's sweet to him.'

They talked for a little while longer and then

Fatty got up and shook the crumbs off himself. 'Well, thanks for letting us picnic with you, Mr James,' he said. 'We'll have to be going now. Are you coming too?'

'No. I'll sit here a bit longer,' said John James. 'There's going to be a grand sunset later on.'

The Find-Outers went down the hill, with Buster capering along on his short legs. 'Well,' said Fatty, when they were out of hearing, 'John James is out of our list of suspects. His alibi is first rate. He was in the cinema all right on Friday evening. Gosh, this mystery is getting deeper and deeper. I'm stumped!'

'Oh *no*, Fatty,' said Bets, quite shocked to hear Fatty say this. 'You *can't* be stumped! Not with your wonderful brains!'

20. DEFEAT – AND A BRAINWAVE

Fatty racked his brains that night, but to no effect. However much he thought and thought, he could see no solution to the mystery at all. He was certain Boysie hadn't done the job. He was also quite certain that Zoe, whose alibi was a little shaky, had had nothing to do with it either. Everyone else had unshakeable alibis. It was true they hadn't checked Alec Grant's, but Fatty had looked up a local paper and had seen a report of the one-man concert that Alec had given on the Friday evening at Sheepridge.

'The report in the paper is a good enough alibi,' he said to the others. 'We needn't bother any more about Alec. But WHO is the culprit? Who did the job?'

In desperation, he went down that evening to talk to PC Pippin. He was there, walking up and down Mr Goon's little back garden, smoking a pipe. He was pleased to see Fatty.

'Any news?' said Fatty. 'I suppose Mr Goon's out?'

'Yes, thank goodness,' said Pippin, feelingly. 'He's been at me all day long about something or other. Pops in and out on that bike of his, and doesn't give me any peace at all. He's gone down to see Boysie again now. I'm very much afraid he'll scare him into a false confession.'

'Yes, I'm afraid of that too,' said Fatty. 'What about Zoe? Does Mr Goon think she had anything to do with it?'

'I'm afraid he does,' said Pippin. 'He's got that handkerchief of hers with Z on, you know – that's one of his main pieces of evidence.'

'But that's nonsense!' said Fatty. 'The handkerchief might have been on that verandah for days! It doesn't prove she was there that night.'

'Goon thinks it does,' said Pippin. 'You see, he has found out that the cleaner swept that verandah clean on Friday afternoon at four o'clock! So the hanky must have been dropped after that.'

Fatty bit his lip and frowned. That was very bad indeed. He hadn't known that. Of *course* Mr Goon thought Zoe had crept to that verandah that evening and been let in by Boysie, if he found a hanky there with a Z on it – a hanky which must have been dropped after four o'clock! That was a very nasty bit of evidence indeed.

'What annoys Mr Goon is that Zoe keeps on denying it's her hanky,' said Pippin. 'Says she's never seen it before. It's a pity it's got Z on it – such an unusual initial.'

'I know,' groaned poor Fatty, feeling very much inclined to make a clean breast of how he had planted the handkerchief and all the other 'clues' on the verandah himself. Well – if Mr Goon did arrest Zoe and Boysie, he would certainly *have* to own up. He turned to Pippin.

'Telephone me Mr Pippin, if you hear any serious news – such as Mr Goon getting a false confession from Boysie – or making an arrest,' he said.

Pippin nodded. 'I certainly will. What have *you* been doing about the mystery? I bet you haven't been idle!'

Fatty told him how he had checked up all the alibis and found them unshakeable – except for Zoe's. He was feeling very worried indeed. It would be awful if Mr Goon solved the mystery the wrong way – and got the wrong people! If only Fatty could see a bit of daylight. But he couldn't.

He went back home, quite depressed, which was very unusual for Fatty. Larry telephoned him that evening to find out if he had heard anything fresh from PC Pippin.

Fatty told him all he knew. Larry listened in silence.

For once, Fatty was completely at a loss. There didn't seem anything to do at all. 'I don't see *what* we can do,' he said miserably. 'I'm absolutely stuck. Fat lot of good we are at detecting! We'll have to break up the Find-Outers if we can't do better than this.'

'Come up at ten tomorrow and have a meeting,' said Larry. 'We'll all think hard and talk and go over absolutely *every*thing. There's something we've missed, I'm sure – some idea we haven't thought of. There's no mystery without a solution, Fatty. Cheer up. We'll find it!'

But before ten o'clock the next day, the telephone rang, and PC Pippin relayed some very bad news to Fatty.

'Are you there? I've only got a minute. Mr Goon has got a confession from Boysie! And Zoe's in it too! Apparently Boysie said he and Zoe worked the thing together. He let Zoe in at the verandah door, they made the tea, Boysie took the cup up with the dope in to the manager – then when he fell asleep, Zoe went up and robbed the safe. She apparently knew where the key was and everything.'

Fatty listened in horror. 'But, Mr Pippin! *Mr Pippin*! Boysie couldn't have done it – nor could Zoe. Mr Goon's *forced* that confession out of a poor fellow who's so confused in his head he doesn't really know what he's saying.'

There was a pause. 'Well, I'm inclined to agree with you,' said Pippin. 'In fact – well, I shouldn't tell you this, but I must – I think from what Mr Goon has let slip, he *did* force that false confession from Boysie, poor wretch. Now, see here, I'm helpless. I can't go against Goon. You're the only one that can do anything. Isn't Inspector Jenks a *great* friend of yours? Won't he believe what you say, if you tell him you think there's been a mistake?'

'But I haven't any *proof*,' wailed Fatty. 'Now, if I *knew* who the robber was, and could produce him, with real evidence, the Inspector would listen to me like a shot. I'll go and see the others, and see what they think. If we can't think of anything better, I'll cycle over to the next town and see the Inspector myself.'

'Well, you'd better make . . .' began PC Pippin, and then Fatty heard the receiver being put back with a click. He guessed that Mr Goon had come in. He sat by the telephone and thought hard. This was frightful! Poor Zoe. Poor Boysie. What in the world could he do to help them?

He tore off to Pip's on his bicycle. The others were there already. They looked gloomy – and they looked gloomier still when Fatty told them what PC Pippin had said.

'It's serious,' said Larry. 'More serious than any other mystery we've tackled. What can we do, Fatty?'

'We'll go through all the suspects and the alibis, and run through all we know,' said Fatty, getting out his notebook. 'I've got everything down here. Listen while I read it – and think, think, think *hard* all the time. As Larry says – we've missed something – some clue, or some evidence, that will help us. There's something very wrong, and probably the explanation is sticking out a mile – if we could only *see* it!'

He began to read through his notes – the list of

suspects. The alibi they had each given. The checking of all the alibis. Boysie's account of the evening of the crime. The manager's own account. The dislike that each member of the show felt for the manager, which would give each one of them a motive for paying him back. Everything in his notebook Fatty read out, clearly and slowly, and the Find-Outers listened intently, even Buster sitting still with ears cocked.

He finished. There was a long pause. Fatty looked up. 'Any suggestions?' he asked, not very hopefully.

The others shook their heads. Fatty shut his notebook with a snap. 'Defeated!' he said bitterly. 'Beaten! All we know is that out of the seven people who are suspects, the two who *could* have done it, didn't – Boysie and Zoe – we *know* they didn't. They're incapable of doing such a thing. And the others, who *might* have done it, all have first class alibis. How *can* the pantomime cat have done the deed when it isn't in his nature to do it?'

'It almost makes you think it must have been somebody else in Boysie's skin,' said Bets.

The others laughed scornfully. 'Silly!' said Pip, and Bets went red.

And then Fatty went suddenly and inexplicably mad. He stared at Bets with fixed and glassy eyes. Then he smacked her on the shoulder. Then he got up and did a solemn and ridiculous dance round the room, looking as if he was in the seventh heaven of delight.

'Bets!' he said, stopping at last. '*Bets*! Good, clever, brainy old Bets. She's got it! She's solved it! Bets, you deserve to be head of the Find-Outers! Oh my word, Bets, why, why, why didn't I think of it before?'

The others all stared at him as if he was out of his mind. 'Fatty, don't be an idiot. Tell us what you mean,' said Pip, crossly. 'What's Bets been so clever about? For the life of me I don't know!'

'Nor do I,' said Larry. 'Sit down Fatty, and explain.'

Fatty sat down, beaming all over his face. He put his arm round the astonished Bets and squeezed her. 'Dear old Bets – she's saved Boysie and Zoe. What brains!'

'*Fatty*! Shut up and tell us what you mean!' almost yelled Pip in exasperation.

'Right,' said Fatty. 'You heard what young Bets said, didn't you? She said, "It almost makes you think it must have been somebody else in Boysie's skin". Well? Well, I ask you? Can't you see that's the solution? Turnip-heads, you don't see it yet!'

'I'm beginning to see,' said Larry slowly. 'But you see it *all*, Fatty, obviously. Tell us.'

'Now, look here,' said Fatty. 'Boysie says he did *not* take the tea in to the manager, doesn't he? But the manager swears he *did*. And why does he swear that? Because Boysie, he says, was wearing his cat-skin. All right. Whoever brought the tea was certainly the pantomime cat – but as the manager never saw who was *inside* the skin, how does he know it was Boysie?'

The others listened in amazement.

'And as it happens, it *wasn't* Boysie!' said Fatty, triumphantly. 'Let me tell you what *I* think happened that night, now that Bets has opened my eyes.'

'Yes, go on, tell us,' said Pip, getting excited as he too began to see what Fatty was getting at.

'Well – the theatre cast all departed, as we know, at half past five, because we saw them go,' said Fatty. 'Only Boysie was left, because he lives there, and the manager was upstairs in his office.

'Now, there was a member of the cast who had a

grudge against the manager, and wanted to pay him back. So that night, after *we* had gone home from our planting of false clues, this person came silently back – let himself in secretly, because Boysie didn't see him or he would have said so – and hid till he saw Boysie making the tea. He knew that Boysie always made tea and took a cup to the manager.

'Very well. Boysie made the tea, and poured himself out a cup. But he didn't drink it because it was too hot. He waited till it was cooler. And the hidden person slipped out, and put a sleeping-draught into Boysie's cup.

'Boysie drank it, felt terribly sleepy, went into the verandah room and snored by the fire. The hidden person then made sure that Boysie was doped and wouldn't wake up – and he *stripped the skin off Boysie . . .*'

'And put it on himself!' cried all the others together. 'Oh, *Fatty*!'

'Yes – he put it on himself. And made a cup of tea for the manager, putting into it a sleeping-draught, of course – and up the stairs he went! Well, how could the manager guess it was anyone but Boysie in his pantomime cat-skin! Wouldn't *anyone* think that?'

'Of course,' said Daisy. 'And then he waited till the manager had drunk his tea and fallen asleep – and did the robbery!'

'Exactly,' said Fatty. 'Took down the mirror, found the key in the manager's wallet, worked out the combination that would open the safe – and stole everything in it. Then he went down to the sleeping Boysie and pulled him into the skin again – and departed as secretly as he came, with the money!

'He knew that when the cup of tea was examined and traces of a sleeping-draught were found, the first question asked would be, "*Who* brought up the cup of tea to the manager?"' said Fatty. 'And the answer to that – quite untruly as it happens – was, of course, Boysie.'

'Oh, Fatty – it's wonderful,' said Bets, her face shining. 'We've solved the mystery!'

'We haven't,' said Larry and Pip together.

'We *have*,' said Bets indignantly.

'Ah, wait a minute, Bets,' said Fatty. 'We know how the thing was done – but the *real* mystery now is – *who was inside the skin of the pantomime cat?*'

21. THE LAST ALIBI IS CHECKED

Everyone felt tremendously excited. Larry smacked Bets proudly on the back. 'You just hit the nail on the head, Bets, when you made that brainy remark of yours,' he said.

'Well – I didn't know it was brainy,' said Bets. 'I just said it without thinking really.'

'I *told* you there was something sticking out a mile, right under our very noses,' said Fatty. 'And that was it. Come on now – we've got to find out who was in the skin.'

They all thought. 'But what's the good of thinking it's this person or that person?' said Pip at last. 'If we say "John James", for instance, it can't be, because we've checked his alibi and it's perfect.'

'Let's not worry about alibis,' said Fatty. 'Once we decide who the person was inside the cat-skin, we'll recheck the alibi – and, what's more, we'll then find it's false! It must be. Come on now – who was inside that cat-skin?'

'Not John James,' said Daisy. 'He was much too big – too fat.'

'Yes – it would have to be a small person,' said Fatty. 'Boysie is small, and only a person about his size could wear that skin.'

They all ran their minds over the members of the cast. Larry thumped on the floor.

'Alec Grant! He's the smallest of the lot – very neat and dapper and slim – don't you remember?'

'Yes! The others are *all* too big – even the two girls, who are too tall to fit the skin,' said Fatty. 'Alec Grant is the only member who could possibly get into the skin.'

'*And* he split it!' said Daisy suddenly. 'Oh, don't you remember, Fatty, how Boysie came and asked Zoe to mend it for him – and she looked at the splitting seams and said he must be getting bigger? Well, he wasn't! Somebody bigger than he was had used his skin and split it!'

'Gosh, yes,' said Fatty. 'Would you believe it – a clue as big as that staring us in the face and we never noticed it! But I say – *Alec Grant*?

He's got the best alibi of the whole lot.'

'He certainly has,' said Larry. 'It's going to be a hard alibi to break too. Impossible, it seems to me.'

'No. Not impossible,' said Fatty. 'He couldn't be in two places at once. And so, if he was in the pantomime cat's skin at the Little Theatre on Friday evening, he was *not* giving a concert at Sheepridge! That's certain.'

'Fancy! The only alibi we didn't check,' said Larry.

'Yes – and I *said* that a good detective always checks everything, whether he thinks it is necessary or not,' groaned Fatty. 'I must be going downhill rapidly. I consider I've done very badly over this!'

'You haven't, Fatty,' said Bets. 'Why, it was you who saw that my remark, which was really only a joke, was the real clue to the mystery! I didn't see that, and nor did the others.'

'How are we going to shake this alibi of Alec Grant's?' said Larry. 'Let's keep to the subject. We haven't much time, it seems to me, if Mr Goon has got a false confession from poor Boysie. He'll be getting in touch with the Inspector any time now and making an arrest – two arrests, I suppose, if Zoe has to be in it too.'

'Anyone got friends in Sheepridge?' asked Fatty suddenly.

'I've got a cousin there – you know him, Freddie Wilson,' said Larry. 'Why?'

'Well, I suppose there's a chance he might have gone to Alec's concert,' said Fatty. 'Telephone him and see, Larry. We've got to find out something about this concert now.'

'*Freddie* won't have gone to a concert like that – to see a man impersonating women,' said Larry, scornfully.

'Go and phone him,' said Fatty. 'Ask him if he knows anything about it.'

Larry went, rather reluctantly. He was afraid that Freddie would jeer at his inquiry.

But Freddie was out and it was his eighteen-year-old sister, Julia, who answered. And she provided an enormous bit of luck!

'No, Larry, Freddie didn't go,' she said. 'Can you see him going to *any* kind of concert? I can't. But I went with Mother. Alec Grant was awfully good – honestly, you couldn't have told he was a man. I waited afterwards and got his autograph.'

'Hold on a minute,' said Larry, and went to

report to Fatty. Fatty leapt up as if he had been shot. 'Got his *autograph*! Gosh – this is super. Don't you remember, idiot, *we've* all got his autograph too! I'd like to see the autograph *Julia* got! I'll eat my hat if it isn't quite different from the one *we've* got!'

'But Fatty – Alec Grant was there, giving the concert,' began Larry. 'Julia says so.'

Fatty took absolutely no notice of him but rushed to the telephone, with Buster excitedly at his heels, feeling that there really must be something up!

'Julia! Frederick Trotteville here. *Could* I come over and see you by the next bus? Most important. Will you be in?'

Julia laughed at Fatty's urgent voice. 'Oh, Frederick – you sound as if you're in the middle of a mystery or something. Yes, of course. Come over. I'll be most interested to know what you want!'

Fatty put down the receiver and rushed back to the others. 'I'm off to Sheepridge,' he said. 'Coming, anyone?'

'Of *course*,' said everyone at once. What! Be left out just when things were getting so thrilling! No, everyone was determined to be in at the death.

They arrived at Sheepridge an hour later, and went to find Julia. She was waiting for them, and was amused to see all five march in.

'Listen, Julia,' began Fatty. 'I can't explain everything to you now – it would take too long – but we are very curious about Alec Grant. You say he really was there, performing at the concert? You actually recognized him, and have seen him before?'

'Yes. Of course I recognised him,' said Julia.

Fatty felt a little taken aback. He had hoped Julia would say she didn't recognise him, and then he might be able to prove that somebody else had taken Alec's place.

'Have you your autograph album with his signature in?' he asked. Julia went to get it. All the Find-Outers had brought theirs with them, and Fatty silently compared the five signatures in their books with the one in Julia's.

Julia's was utterly and entirely different!

'Look,' said Fatty, pointing. 'The autographs he did for us are illegible squiggles – the one he did for Julia is perfectly clear and readable. It *wasn't* Alec Grant who did that!'

'You'll be saying it was his twin-sister next,' said Julia with a laugh.

Fatty stared as if he couldn't believe his ears. 'What did you say?' he almost shouted. '*Twin-sister*, Julia? – you don't really mean to say he's got a twin-sister?'

'Of course he has,' said Julia. 'What *is* all this mystery about? I've seen his sister – exactly like him, small and neat. She doesn't live here, she lives at Marlow.'

Fatty let out an enormous sigh. 'Why didn't I think of a twin?' he said. 'Of course! The *only* solution! He got his twin to come and do his show for him. Is she good too, Julia?'

'Well, they're both in shows,' said Julia. 'As a matter-of-fact, Alec is supposed to be much better than Nora, his sister. I thought he wasn't so good last Friday really – he had such a terrible cold, for one thing, and kept stopping to cough.'

The others immediately looked at one another. Oh! A cough and a cold! Certainly Alec hadn't had one on Monday afternoon when they had all heard him sing. Nobody had seen any sign of a cold or cough then. Very, very suspicious!

'May we take this album away for a little while?' asked Fatty. 'I'll send it back. Thanks so much for seeing us. You've been a great help.'

'I don't know how,' said Julia. 'It seems very mysterious to me.'

'It *has* been very mysterious,' said Fatty, preparing to go. 'Very, very mysterious. But I see daylight now, though I very – nearly – didn't!'

The Five Find-Outers went off with Buster, excited and talkative. 'We've got it all straightened out now,' said Fatty happily. 'Thanks to Bets. Honestly Bets, we'd have been absolutely stumped if you hadn't made that sudden remark. It was a brainwave.'

They got back to Peterswood, having decided what to do. They would go and see PC Pippin first, and tell him all they knew. Fatty said they owed it to him to do that, and if he wanted to arrest Alec Grant, he could. What a shock for Mr Goon!

But when they got to Mr Goon's house, they had a shock. PC Pippin was there alone, looking very gloomy.

'Ah, Frederick,' he said, when he saw Fatty, 'I've been trying to telephone you for the last hour. Mr

Goon's arrested Boysie and Zoe, and they're both in an awful state! I'm afraid Boysie will go right off his head now.'

'Where are they?' asked Fatty, desperately.

'Goon's taken them over to the Inspector,' said PC Pippin. 'What's the matter with *you*? You look all of a dither.'

'I am,' said Fatty, sitting down suddenly. 'Mr Pippin, listen hard to what I'm going to tell you. And then tell us what to do. Prepare for some shocks. Now – listen!'

22. A SURPRISE FOR THE INSPECTOR!

Pippin listened, his eyes almost falling out of his head. He heard about the false clues and frowned. He heard about the way the children had interviewed the suspects by means of asking for autographs – he heard about the tea party – the checking up of the alibis – and then he heard about Bets' bright remark that had suddenly set Fatty on the right track.

The autograph albums were produced and compared. The visit to Sheepridge related. The twin-sister came into the story, and PC Pippin rubbed his forehead in bewilderment as Fatty produced the many, many pieces of the jigsaw puzzle that, all fitted together, made a clear solution to the mystery.

'Well! I don't know what to think,' said poor PC Pippin. 'This beats me! Mr Goon's got the wrong ones, no doubt about that. And I think there's no doubt that Alec Grant is the culprit.'

'Can you arrest him then and take him to the Inspector?' cried Fatty.

'No. Of course not,' said Pippin. 'Not just on what you've told me. But I'll tell you what we *can* do – I can go and detain him for questioning. I can take him over to the Inspector and face him with all you've said.'

'Oh *yes* – that's a fine idea,' said Fatty. 'Can we come too?'

'You'll have to,' said PC Pippin. 'My word, I shan't like to look at the Inspector's face when he hears about those false clues of yours. Good thing you've solved the mystery, that's all I can say. Let's hope that will cancel out the mischief you got into first.'

Pippin's voice was stern, but his eyes twinkled. 'Can't be really cross with you myself,' he said. 'Your clues put me where I could see the crime when it was just done – and now it looks as if I'll be able to show Mr Goon up. He deserves it, brow-beating that poor, simple-headed fellow into a false confession!'

The morning went on being more and more

exciting. Alec Grant was collected from the theatre, where he was rehearsing with the others, who were most alarmed at Zoe's arrest. He put on a very bold face and pretended that he hadn't the least idea why Pippin wanted to question him.

He was very surprised to see all the children also crammed into the big car that Pippin had hired to take them over to see the Inspector. But nobody explained anything to him. The children looked away from him. Horrid, beastly thief – and how *could* he let Zoe and Boysie take the blame for something he himself had done?

Pippin telephoned the Inspector before they left. 'Sir? Pippin here. About that Little Theatre job. I believe Mr Goon's brought his two arrests over to you. Well, sir, can you hold things up for a bit? I've got some fresh evidence here, sir. Very important. I'm bringing someone over to question – man named Alec Grant. Also, sir, I'm bringing – er – five children.'

'What?' said Inspector Jenks, thinking he must have misheard. 'Five *what*?'

'CHILDREN, sir,' said Pippin. 'You know, sir, you told me about them before I came here. One's a boy called Frederick Trotteville.'

'Oh, *really*?' said the Inspector. 'That's most interesting. So he's been working on this too, has he? Do you know what conclusions he has come to Pippin?'

'Yes, sir, I know all about it,' said Pippin. 'Er – Mr Goon didn't want me to work with him on this case, sir, so – er – well . . .'

'So you worked with Frederick, I suppose,' said the Inspector. 'Very wise of you. Well – I'll hold things up till you come.'

He called Mr Goon into his room. 'Er, Goon,' he said, 'we must wait for about twenty minutes before proceeding with anything. Pippin has just phoned through. He's got fresh evidence.'

Goon bristled like a hedgehog. 'Pippin, sir? He doesn't know a thing about this case. Not a thing. I wouldn't let him work with me on it, he's such a turnip-head. Course, he's only been with me a little while, but it's easy to see he's not going to be much good. Not enough brains. And a bit too cocky, sir, if you'll excuse the slang.'

'Certainly,' said the Inspector. 'Well, we will wait. Pippin is bringing a man for questioning.'

Goon's mouth fell open. 'A man – for

questioning? But we've *got* the people who did the job. What's he want to bring a man for? Who is it?'

'And he's also bringing five children, he says,' went on the Inspector, enjoying himself very much, for he did not like the domineering, conceited Mr Goon. 'One of them is, I believe, that clever boy – the one who has helped us with so many mysteries – Frederick Trotteville!'

Goon opened and shut his mouth like a goldfish and for two minutes couldn't say a single word. He went slowly purple and the Inspector looked at him in alarm.

'You'll have a heart attack one of these days, Goon, if you get so angry,' he said. 'Surely you don't mind Frederick coming over? You are quite sure you have solved the case yourself, and arrested the right people – so what is there to worry about?'

'I'm not worrying,' said Goon, fiercely. 'That boy – always interfering with the law – always . . .'

'Now Goon, he *helps* the law, he doesn't interfere with it,' said the Inspector.

Goon muttered something about turnip-heads, and then subsided into deep gloom. Pippin coming – and all those dratted children! What was up?

Pippin duly arrived with Alec Grant, the five children, and, of course, Buster. Goon's face grew even blacker when he saw Buster, who greeted him with frantic joy, as if he was an old friend, tearing round his feet in a most exasperating way.

'Ah, Frederick – so you're on the job again,' said the Inspector. 'Pleased to see you. Hello, Larry – Pip – Daisy – and here's little Bets too. Have they turned you out of the Find-Outers yet, Bets?'

'Turned her out! I should think not,' said Fatty. 'If it hadn't been for Bets, we'd never have hit on the right solution.'

There was a growl from Goon at this. The Inspector turned to him. 'Ah, Goon – you also think you have hit on the right solution, don't you?' he said. 'Your two arrests are in the other room. Now – what makes you think you have solved the case correctly, Goon? You were just about to tell me when I got Pippin's telephone call.'

'Sir, there's a confession here from Boysie Summers, the pantomime cat,' said Goon. 'Says as clear as a pikestaff that he did the job, with Zoe Markham to help him. This here's her handkerchief, found on the verandah on the night of the crime – Z for Zoe, in the corner, sir.'

'Oh!' said Daisy. 'That's *my* old hanky, Inspector! And I put the Z in the corner, just for a joke. Didn't I, you others?'

The other four nodded at once. 'It's certainly not Zoe's,' said Daisy. 'She'd never have a dirty, torn old hanky like this. I should have thought Mr Goon would have guessed that.'

Mr Goon began to breathe heavily. 'Now look here!' he began.

'Wait, Goon,' said the Inspector, picking up the 'confession'. 'So this is what Boysie said, is it? Bring him in, please Pippin. He and Zoe are in the next room. They can both come in.'

Pippin went to fetch Zoe and Boysie. Zoe was in tears, and so upset that she didn't even seem to see the five children. She went straight up to the Inspector and tapped the 'confession' he held in his hand.

'Not one word of that is true!' she said. 'Not one word! *He* forced Boysie to say things that weren't true. Look at Boysie – can you imagine him doing a crime like that even with my help? He's nothing but a child, even though he's twenty-four. That policeman badgered him and terrified him and threatened him till poor Boysie was so frightened he said anything. Anything! It's wicked, really *wicked*!'

Boysie stood beside her. The children hardly knew him, out of his cat-skin. He did seem only a child – a child that trembled and shook and clutched at Zoe's dress. Bets felt the tears coming into her eyes.

'Well, Miss Markham,' said Inspector Jenks, 'we have here someone else for questioning. I think you know him.'

Zoe turned and saw Alec. 'Alec Grant!' she said. 'Did *you* do it, Alec? Alec, if you did, say so. Would you let poor Boysie be sent *right* off his head with this, if you could help it? You hated the manager. You always said so. Did *you* do it?'

Alec said nothing. The Inspector turned to Pippin. 'Pippin – will you say why you have brought this man here, please?'

Pippin began his tale. He told it extremely well and lucidly. It was plain to see that PC Pippin would one day make a very good policeman indeed!

The Inspector interrupted occasionally to ask a

question, and sometimes Fatty had to put a few words in too. Goon sat with his mouth open, his eyes almost bulging out of his head.

Alec Grant looked more and more uncomfortable as time went on. When Pippin and Fatty between them related how the children had gone to Sheepridge and seen the different autograph in Julia's album – which Pippin placed before the Inspector as evidence – he turned very pale.

'So you think this man here got his twin-sister to impersonate him, while he slipped back to the theatre, doped Boysie, got into the cat-skin, took up a doped cup of tea to the manager, robbed the safe, and then pulled the skin on the sleeping Boysie again?' said Inspector Jenks. 'A most ingenious crime. We must get on to the man's twin-sister. We must bring her in too.'

'Here!' said Goon, in a strangled sort of voice. 'I can't have this. I tell you that man's not the culprit – he *didn't* do it. Haven't I got that confession there for you to see?'

And then poor Goon got a terrible shock. 'I *did* do it!' said Alec Grant. 'Exactly as PC Pippin described it. But leave my sister out of it, *please*! She knows nothing about it at all! I telephoned her and begged her to take my place at the concert, and she did. She's done that before when I've felt ill, and nobody has known. We're as alike as peas. I impersonate women, as you know – and who's to know the difference if my sister impersonates *me*? No one! Only these kids – they're too clever by half!'

Inspector Jenks took the 'confession' and tore it in half. 'There's a fire behind you, Goon,' he said, in a cold voice. 'Put this in, will you?'

And Goon had to put the wonderful 'confession' into the fire and watch it burn. He wished he could sink through the floor. He wished he was at the other end of the world. If ever cruelty and stupidity and conceit were punished well and truly, then they were punished now, in the person of Goon.

'I've got all the money,' said Alec. 'I meant to give it back really. It was just to give the manager a nasty shock – he's a mean old beast. If I'd known Boysie and Zoe had been arrested I'd have owned up.'

'You *did* know,' said Pippin quietly. 'No good saying that now.'

'Well,' said the Inspector, leaning back and

looking at the children. 'Well! Once more you appear to have come to our rescue, children. I'm much obliged to you, Pippin, my congratulations – you handled this case well, in spite of being forbidden to work with Goon. Frederick, you are incorrigible and irrepressible – and if you place any more false clues, I shall probably be forced to arrest you! You are also a very great help, and most ingenious in your tackling of any problem. Thanks very much!'

The Inspector beamed round at the five children and Pippin, including Zoe and Boysie in his smile. Bets slipped her hand into his. 'You don't *really* mean you'd arrest Fatty?' she said anxiously. 'We were all as bad as he was with those clues and things, Inspector.'

'No. I was pulling his leg,' said the Inspector. 'Not that I approve of that sort of behaviour at all, you understand – very reprehensible indeed – but I can't help feeling that what you all did later has quite cancelled out what came before! And now, do you know what time it is? Two o'clock. Has anyone had any lunch?'

Nobody had, and the children suddenly became

aware of a very hollow feeling in their middles.

'Well, I hope you will do me the honour of lunching with me at the Royal Hotel,' said the Inspector. 'I'll get someone to telephone your families, who will no doubt be searching the countryside for you now! And perhaps Miss Zoe would come too – and, er, – the pantomime cat?'

'Oh, thank you,' said Zoe, all smiles. 'Are we quite free now?'

'Quite,' said the Inspector. 'Goon, take this fellow Grant away. And wait here till I come back. I shall have a few words to say to you.'

Goon, looking like a pricked balloon, took Alec Grant away. Bets heaved a sigh of relief. 'Oh, Inspector Jenks, I was *so* afraid you'd ask Mr Goon to come out to lunch too!'

'Not on your life!' said the Inspector. 'Oh, you're there too, PC Pippin. Go and get yourself a good meal in the police station canteen, and then come back here and write out a full report of this case for me. And ring the children's parents, will you?'

Pippin saluted and grinned. He was very pleased with himself. He winked at Fatty and Fatty winked back. Aha! There would be a spot of promotion for

Pippin if he went on handling cases like this.

'I've really enjoyed this mystery,' said Bets, as she sat down at a hotel table and unfolded a snowy white napkin. 'It was very, very difficult – but it wasn't frightening at all.'

'Oh yes it was – to me and Boysie,' said Zoe. She filled a glass with lemonade and held it up to the children.

'Here's to you!' she cried. 'The Five Find-Outers – and Dog!'

The Inspector raised his glass too, and grinned. 'Here's to the great detectives – who solved the insoluble and most mysterious case in their career – the Mystery of the Pantomime Cat!'